THE IMMORTALS

THE IMMORTALS

RALPH MILNE FARLEY

ILLUSTRATED BY
SAMUEL CAHAN

COVER BY
ROBERT A. GRAEF

POPULAR PUBLICATIONS · 2022

TABLE OF CONTENTS

THE IMMORTALS

An eminent young chemist discovers a new element, "Stratium," in his laboratory— then finds his rival's dead body

1

THE SINISTER RACE

A BROAD-SHOULDERED, SANDY-HAIRED young man sat with other persons in the waiting room of the Wall Street brokerage office of Diggs & Co. In his hands was a morning newspaper. From time to time he glanced aimlessly at the front page headlines: something about a gang-murder and a kidnapping.

What were murders and kidnappings to him? His specialty was science, not crime. And yet there were features about this particular murder, and this particular kidnapping, which attracted even his attention. Both trails had led to the waters of New York harbor. Not to any boat, but to the bare water, into which the suspects had run and never come up, with the police hot on their trail! Nor had any bodies been found.

Then, with an amused shrug at the pose which it involved, the young man turned to the financial page. And there a small headline really did attract his attention: "Diggs Stocks Being Pounded." He read on. The article stated that the Diggs group had been caught short by the Maitland group; but the financial editor expressed the belief that, as usual, Wolf Diggs would be able to extricate himself and his friends.

The young scientist hoped that the financial editor was

*He stepped slowly
and preciesely
toward the body*

right; for, although these Wall Street wars touched him as little as did gang-murders and kidnappings, nevertheless Wolf Diggs was his patron, the man who was financing his researches in atomic physics.

HIS READING WAS interrupted by a voice which was saying, "Mr. Deane, Mr. Diggs will see you now. Please step this way."

Rising, Deane followed the frock-coated, male secretary who had made the announcement. Through a high oak-paneled door they passed into a smaller room, containing a single desk (quite obviously unused) and several chairs.

The young scientist sat down in one of the chairs, and smoothed his tousled hair with one hand; then glanced around the room. It was oak-paneled, with three doors. One was the door through which he had entered. The secretary had departed through the second. The third door bore, in letters of gold, the simple inscription: "Mr. Diggs."

As Deane gazed at it, he heard beyond it what sounded like the sharp crack of a pistol. Then a dull thud against the door, which swung partly open at the sound.

For a moment, Deane stared in surprise; then jumped to his feet, strode to the door, and swung it open all the way.

There lay the well-known figure of Wolf Diggs, an automatic pistol clutched in his right hand, and a spreading blob of reddish brown on his shirt front. As Deane looked, the fingers of the dying man relaxed and let go the weapon. He coughed. Pink froth flecked his lips.

Deane glanced hurriedly around the room. The window was open, and as he looked in its direction, he thought he saw the back of a man's head just disappearing to one side beyond the window. Deane dashed over and peered out. But there was no one there; so he returned and bent over the prostrate banker.

Doors opened. Feet came running.

Together Deane and the secretary lifted the body and laid it on a leather couch in the inner office.

"Don't touch the gun," cautioned Deane to the employees of the firm.

"Everyone get out of here, except Mr. Deane and me,"
the secretary commanded. "Miss Jones, bring some water
quickly. Mr. Laflin, telephone for the doctor on the sixth
floor, and then notify the police."

The hushed crowd moved from the room. But just as the
last of them left, Deane heard someone say, "And sell our
stocks short, before Maitland learns of this!"

Then a veritable scramble began.

The water came. Deane raised the shoulders of the dying
broker, and the secretary held the glass of water.

The wounded man took a gulp, then heaved his chest
and tried to speak.

"He—got—me!"

"Who?" demanded the secretary. "Tell us who got you,
sir."

"Maitland got me," whispered Diggs.

Then his head flopped gruesomely to one side, and his
whole body relaxed in Deane's arms.

"It's no use," said the secretary sadly and yet a bit proudly.
"He was thinking of the market, rather than about his own
impending death."

Deane arranged the body on the couch, and stood up.
Together he and the secretary surveyed in silence what had
been Wolf Diggs, master of Wall Street, patron to one of
them, loved employer of the other.

The doctor came; but there was nothing he could do, for
Wolf Diggs was dead.

Then arrived a police inspector, who wrapped the gun

carefully in a clean handkerchief, and pocketed it; and then questioned Deane and the secretary at considerable length.

"Name and occupation?"

"Charles Deane, research chemist."

"Hm. Any relation to the Columbia football star?"

"I played on the Columbia team three years ago."

"Well, well! Glad to know you," said the detective, holding out his hand. "I saw you play that time you trimmed Yale."

And from then on his attitude was decidedly friendly.

He continued, "What you been doing since you left Columbia?"

"Postgraduate work at Johns Hopkins. Atomic physics and electron theory."

"You can search me," said the policeman, grinning. "Well, how come you were here today?"

"Mr. Diggs was interested in my work at Baltimore. So when I got my Ph.D. there, he set me up in a laboratory here in New York for some special experimental work. I was here today to report progress, and to arrange for a further appropriation."

"Well, I'm afraid that's all off now," said the official sympathetically.

"It looks that way."

Deane then told about being in the waiting room, hearing the shot, and so forth.

Finally he was dismissed, and the detective began an interrogation of Diggs's secretary.

AS THE SANDY-HAIRED athlete passed through the outer office of the brokerage firm, he found everything in confusion, with the bottom dropping out of the stock market.

Outside, the newsboys were already crying an extra on the death of Wolf Diggs, and the collapse of the market. Deane bought several papers, and read them in the subway, on his way to the office-building which housed his laboratory.

Most of the accounts treated the death as a suicide; but one of the tabloids hinted that it might be murder, the culmination of a long series of recent unexplained crimes which had nearly driven to distraction the intense and red-headed young District Attorney of New York County, Dan McGrady.

All the papers, of course, played-up the collapse of the market, and what this would mean to John Cortlandt Maitland, chief financial rival to the now-deceased Wolf Diggs. To Maitland it would mean a clean-up; for, as usual, Maitland had been on the other side of the market from Diggs.

Strange—and this again was one of the tabloids—how almost every one of the unexplained crimes of recent months had resulted in some advantage to Maitland, who was of course totally unconnected with any of these outrages, being one of the most thoroughly respectable figures of the social upper-crust of New York City.

But most of these details failed to register on the mind of the broad-shouldered young scientist, so stunned was he by the suddenness of it all.

Neither the crime-wave nor the stock market meant anything to him, for he never read criminal news or detective stories, and he never played the market. He felt but little personal grief at the death of his patron, for old Diggs had an austere and forbidding personality, and Deane had never seen him except briefly and on business.

But the prospect of an impending shortage of funds for his beloved experiments did give him cause for worry. Also he resented the triumph of Maitland, but chiefly from a sense of loyalty to Diggs.

Seated now, white-smocked, at one of the least littered of the workbenches of his laboratory, he ran his fingers thoughtfully through his sandy hair, and scowled, as he continued to read the papers which he had brought with him.

Angus Frazer, his middle-aged Scotch laboratory assistant, came in, newspaper in hand. With friendly concern on his thin features, he stepped over to Deane and placed a fatherly hand on the shoulder of his young employer.

"Sirr," said he, in his rich Scottish burr, "I ken what this means to you, sirr."

"Good old Angus," said Deane, looking up and smiling wryly. "Good loyal old Angus. Always thinking of someone else, and never of yourself. Hasn't it occurred to you, that, when the Diggs money stops, I shan't be able to afford an assistant any more?"

"Yes, it has, sirr. But I give morr concerrn to the expurraments. Do you suppose you could interrest Maitland? I see he made a clean-up out of Diggs's death."

Deane pursed up his lips, and thought for a moment. Then shook his sandy head.

"NO, ANGUS," HE replied. "Who ever heard of Maitland's donating a cent to anything!"

"Weel, it's rrumorred in scientific cirrcles that it was he who financed the expurraments with heavy waterr."

"Heavy water," mused Deane. "Lord Rutherford, greatest British scientist, has been quoted as saying that he considers the discovery of heavy water as being one of the half dozen greatest achievements of physical science of the present century. All kinds of myths have grown up about it."

"I wouldna call them myths, sirr," admonished his assistant. "Call them theorries."

"Theories or myths," Deane retorted. "Who can really believe that, as some alleged scientists assert, the gradual accumulation of heavy water in human veins is what causes old age and death! All we've got to do, then, is to discover some chemical which will combine with, and neutralize, heavy water; and we can all live forever."

"I didna mean to starrt you off on a discussion of heavy waterr. All I wanted was to point out that if Maitland would finance one expurrament, he would finance another; so why not ourrs?"

But again Deane shook his head. "No," said he. "Maitland must have seen, or thought he saw, some chance to make some money out of heavy water, or he would never have taken it up. And, even if he could be persuaded to help us, it wouldn't be loyal to Diggs's memory, for us to approach his financial rival and enemy to finish up the experiments which Diggs made possible. No, we'll have to turn elsewhere. But meanwhile we're all set for the present. Rent paid for six months in advance, and our work on the stratosphere, underwritten by the Diggs Foundation. So let's get going."

Tossing his newspaper into a wastebasket, he got down

from the stool on which he had been sitting, and strode over to another bench.

"Let's see," he continued resolutely. "Suppose you read to me the report which you were writing for the Diggs Foundation, and let's check it over."

Picking up a notebook, Angus Frazer thumbed the pages, and then read aloud, " 'Two large containerrs of comprressed airr, obtained by Prrofessorr Brrigaud on his balloon flight into the strratospherre, deliverred at ourr laborratorry. Liquified some of this airr. Separrated the sample into its varrious gasses by prrogrressive distillation. Tested each gas, to see if it rreacts like samples obtained frrom orrdinarry airr nearr surrface of earrth.'—There followed several pages, detailing the tests applied to the stratosphere samples of oxygen, nitrogen, carbon, dioxide, argon and helium. Then: 'The hydrrogen sample, howeverr, rreacts queerrly. It will not—.'"

Angus Frazer abruptly stopped reading from the notebook, and glanced sharply at Deane. The latter's expression had suddenly changed from absorbed preoccupation, to alert listening—listening, apparently, to something behind and beyond his assistant.

Frazer wheeled around, and followed the direction of Deane's stare. But he saw nothing of interest.

Turning back, he asked, "Whateverr is the matterr, sirr?"

"Someone just opened the corridor door and looked in," Deane hollowly replied.

The old Scot shook his head with a puzzled frown.

"Well, what of it, sirr?" said he. "I'm sair afraid the death of Mr. Diggs has got you a wee bit jitterry, sirr. But cerrtainly no one can be afterr *you*, sirr."

"I suppose not," Deane admitted, sheepishly fingering his disordered hair. "It must be that I'm nervous or something, on account of what I went through this morning. But I *did* actually see the door open, and a man with a hooked nose and black beard peer in."

"You've been rreading too many mysterry storries," laughed the Scot.

Deane ignored this jibe at the fact that he never read anything lighter than chemistry textbooks, and said, "Shut the door, and go on with the notes, Angus. You were saying—"

FRAZER DID AS directed, and then continued: "The hydrrogen sample, howeverr, rreacts queerrly. It will not burrn!"

"That's what has me puzzled, Angus," said Deane, pursing up his lips and fingering his hair. "We've got to determine the reason for that, even if the Diggs money does give out. This stratosphere hydrogen—will—not—burn! Think of that, Angus! Did you ever know hydrogen not to burn? I believe we're on the verge of discovering something. You know, Angus, ever since I learned at college that, as one gets higher and higher above the earth, the oxygen in the air is gradually replaced by hydrogen, I've always wondered why lightning or flaming meteors didn't explode the mixture, especially at the height at which the ratio of oxygen to hydrogen is two-to-one, H_2O, just the right ratio to explode and form water."

"But, sirr," objected the assistant. "The mixture is so rrarrified at that height that it will not ignite, sirr."

Deane smiled. "That's just what my professor told me," said he. "So I, being of a skeptical mind, filled a bell-jar with a two-to-one oxyhydrogen mixture, exhausted it to just the right degree of rarity, shot an electric current through it, and nearly wrecked the laboratory. Never told the professor about my experiment, for I didn't want to have to pay for the damage. Well, let's get going. I want to see why *this* hydrogen won't burn."

So the two friends proceeded with their experiments. Liquifying some of the hydrogen, they placed it in a tank with two platinum electrodes. The electrical conductivity of the liquid registered much higher than it should.

And then they noticed a very surprising phenomenon: the positive electrode was beginning to grow in size.

By the close of the day it had doubled! Yet, when they weighed it, to determine the exact amount of gain, they found instead a slight loss!

The color of the swelled electrode had changed from the dull silver of platinum to a bright silver like chromium, but with a slight brassy glint.

Thinking that the platinum might perhaps have become spongy—which would account for its increase in size and yet slight loss of weight—Deane tried the sample with his knife; but could not even nick it.

Then he filed it with a diamond file. But the filings, which he succeeded in loosening, disappeared! None fell upon the piece of white paper which he spread upon the bench to receive them!

It was now late evening. They had worked straight through. So intense had been their interest, that they had dismissed from their minds all thoughts of the sinister events of the morning. And yet, in spite of their preoccupation, a sort of ominous gloom had hung over the laboratory all day, and had become intensified as evening had drawn on.

And now at last, as Charles Deane looked up from his surprise at the disappearance of the filings which he was scraping from his platinum anode, the laboratory door again stood ajar, and the same bearded hook-nosed face was again peering in malevolently at him. It was instantly withdrawn.

THIS TIME, INSTEAD of merely staring at the strange face, Deane leaped to his feet and sprang across the laboratory to the half-opened door. Flinging it wide, he dashed into the corridor, and glanced hurriedly in both directions. Then stooped, picked up something from the floor, stepped back into his own laboratory again, and closed and locked the door.

As he straightened and turned away from the door, his assistant confronted him.

"Whateverr is the matterr, sirr?" asked the old Scot.

"That face again!"

"And I suppose you found nothing, sirr. It's yourr nerrves, I'm telling you."

"Only this," Deane dryly replied, holding up a handkerchief, spotted with red. "A handkerchief, and wet with fresh blood, at that."

The eyes of Angus Frazer narrowed as he looked intently at the bit of cloth. Then he shook his head with a puzzled frown.

"Not *quite* the rright colorr forr blood," he opined. "Let's see it."

Deane passed it to his assistant. Frazer smelled of it gingerly; then shook his head again.

"Smells morr like hydrrogen perroxide," said he.

"But why should anyone put pink hydrogen peroxide on his handkerchief?"

"Perhaps it's a mixture of H_2O_2 and mercurochrome," Deane suggested. "Let's test it. It may throw some light on why its owner was snooping around our door."

The tests developed the fact that the red substance contained neither hydrogen peroxide nor mercurochrome. Apparently it was some new oxide, with which neither of the two scientists was acquainted. It was not blood. It did not turn darker when it dried. And yet it did contain quite a quantity of red and white blood corpuscles.

Charles Deane and his assistant were stumped.

2

THE MISSING SAMPLE

IT WAS A month later. The sinister bearded face, which had twice peered in through the doorway of Charles Deane's laboratory on the day of the murder of his millionaire patron, had not been seen again. Nor had further analysis developed any hint as to the nature of the "blood" on the handkerchief which the owner of the face had dropped.

Charles Deane hated to be stumped by anything, and so he devoted more time than a mere passing bit of curiosity deserved, to an attempt at mastering the mystery of the peculiar red substance. Some strange persistency—a feeling that there lurked some hidden personal meaning to this "blood"—drove him on; until finally, when he seemed to be almost on the verge of a clue, the small quantity available was used up.

And other queer things began happening around his laboratory. One morning, on arriving unexpectedly early at work, he found the room filled with a white smoke which smelled of flashlight powders.

He changed the lock on the door, the new lock got out of order, and when he took it off to have it mended, he found inside it unmistakable traces of impression-wax.

Articles of his laboratory equipment began to disappear; and, strange to relate, these were always articles of common use, which could not possibly be of any scientific or monetary value to anyone.

But, in spite of all his disturbing preoccupations, Deane had found opportunity to repeat many times his experiment of the electrolytic decomposition of the hydrogen which had been obtained from the stratosphere. He had fathomed the cause of the increase in size and decrease in weight of his platinum anode. Furthermore, he had found that such hydrogen gas as gathered around his cathode, *would* burn.

But his jubilation at these discoveries was overshadowed by worry over the strange happenings in the laboratory. And he had morbidly taken to reading the criminal news in the daily papers. The murder of his patron, Wolf Diggs, still unsolved, had come to constitute a personal menace to him—just why, he could not say.

His nerves were on edge, especially today.

"There it is again, Angus," he whispered, his athletic body nervously tense. "My God, man, didn't you see it? That evil-looking face peering in at us through the doorway!"

"Mr. Deane, sirr," replied the older man, in that soothing tone of voice which one uses toward children and lunatics, "I saw nothing. Hadn't you betterr be dirrecting yourr thoughts to the vurra rreal dangerr that Prrofessorr Cairrns will heckle you at the Chemical Society tonight?"

"I suppose so," Deane listlessly admitted, pushing his sandy hair back from his forehead with a tired gesture. Then, with momentarily returning vigor, "But, I tell you, Angus, I did see that face again!"

Once more listless after his brief flare-up, the young scientist began with absentminded automatism to turn off burners and to disconnect rubber-tubing and electric wires on the workbench in front of him.

Then brightening, as his thoughts shifted to the coming meeting of the Chemical Society, he asked, "Do you really think the old walrus will be there?"

"Of courrse he will, sirr," the Scotsman replied. "He hates you, and so he canna bearr to see a young lad like you crredited wi' the discoverry of a new chemical element."

Deane's clear gray eyes twinkled good-naturedly, as he said, "Well, *I* don't hate *him*, in spite of his virulence. And his apparent hatred of me is entirely impersonal. Professor Cairns is merely the rear-guard of the old order, conducting a losing fight against modern chemistry. No step in advance would be complete without the bitter opposition of men like Cairns. I'll miss quite a kick, if he fails to bristle up at me tonight."

THE TWO CO-WORKERS finished neatening up the bench, took off their smocks, put on their coats and hats, switched out the lights, and stepped into the corridor. As Deane turned from closing and latching the door of his laboratory, he gripped the arm of his assistant.

"There he goes now!" he whispered, pointing down the hallway toward a hunched black-cloaked figure, just slinking around the next turn.

"Who? Prrofessorr Cairrns?" asked Angus Frazer, with simulated calm.

"No. Of course not. That face!" Deane exploded. "Come on!"

And he broke into a run toward the corner around

which the figure
had disappeared.
The Scotsman
followed.

Professor Cairns

But when
they reached
the elevator, the
doors were just
clanging shut.

"Down!"
shouted Deane.

But the eleva-
tor boy shook his
head.

"Next car," he laconically replied, as he threw his lever.

Through the grating, there leered up at Deane and
Frazer, a sinister swarthy face, with beady eyes, hooked
nose, and black beard. Then the car shot down out of sight.

As Deane pushed the button for another car, he turned
to his assistant with, "Now will you believe me?"

"Well, the man cerrtainly did seem to have a face," Frazer
replied, but his solemn expression belied the forced levity
of his words.

THERE WAS AN unusually large attendance at the spring
meeting of the Chemical Society that evening, although
the title of the paper on which Deane was to read was
merely "Stratium"; which word, unexplained, meant nothing.

On the platform sat President Huntington of the Society; three or four gentlemen who were to deliver minor
papers (the "preliminary bouts," as it were); Charles

Deane, his face flushed with impending battle, his sandy hair disordered as usual, and his gray eyes snapping; and Angus Frazer. Frazer was there by Deane's special request, the stated reason being that the Scotsman was entitled to share in the credit of the discovery of stratium.

But there was a further reason beyond mere magnanimity on Deane's part. For Deane well-knew, from past experience, the tactics employed by his old enemy Cairns at such meetings. Cairns never made a frontal attack. Instead, he would usually question some side-issue, some minor point on which the speaker would be apt to be unprepared. And so Deane had arranged for his elderly assistant to be present, with pockets stuffed full of card-catalog references, to support every statement, regardless how minor, to be made in Deane's own address.

While the preliminary papers were being duly delivered, Deane sat back and swept the faces before him with his clear gray eyes. In the third row, on the center aisle, he recognized the round head, long drooping moustaches, small eyes and pugnacious jaw, which had earned for Professor Cairns the sobriquet of "old walrus-face." Deane's heart sped up a few beats, but he smiled down at his professional rival with a show of confidence. Cairns caught the glance and tossed his head with a contemptuous snort.

A young girl, sitting next to Professor Cairns, turned at the sound, and whispered something to him, whereat he snorted again. The girl was dark, slim and erect, with a wistful mouth, uptilted at the corners. Deane had never seen her before. He smiled down at her too; but she stiffened, and looked away.

Embarrassed, Deane continued his survey of the hall. And then his heart skipped several beats. For, seated near the rear, was the face that had three times peered in through his laboratory door, the face which had leered up at him from the descending elevator, a sinister swarthy face, with beady eyes, hooked nose, and black beard.

Deane clutched the arm of Angus Frazer, who occupied the next seat to his right, and whispered, "Do *you* see what *I* see? Just in front of the fifth pillar on the right!"

The old Scotsman glanced in the indicated direction, and then whispered back, "Yes, but what of it? Can't a funny looking mon walk thrrough the halls of an office building, and look in at a half-opened doorr, and go down in the elevatorr, and then happen to attend a meeting of the Chemical Society, without yourr getting all excited overr it?"

"Ordinarily, yes," Deane replied, "but there's something personal in this fellow's look, something personal and menacing."

"Bosh!" returned the Scot. "Cairrns is sufficient menace forr rright now. Pay yourr attention to him forr the prresent!"

Thus bid, Deane shifted his glance to Cairns, and intercepted an interested stare on the part of the slim young girl. She hastily looked away, and this time it was *her* turn to be embarrassed. Somehow this gave Deane a sort of inward satisfaction. He breathed deeply, and then fell to studying his lecture-notes. But from time to time he cast covert glances in the direction of the girl.

THE MEETING DRONED on. Finally the last preliminary paper was concluded, and President Huntington arose, and announced: "We shall now hear from Dr. Charles Deane, one of our youngest members. Most of you have heard him before. His subject tonight is 'Stratium.' Doubtless he will tell you what it means. And now, without further ado, I shall throw him to the lions. Gentlemen, Dr. Deane."

The young chemist arose, clutching a sheaf of lecture-notes in his left hand, ran the fingers of his right hand through his sandy hair, and then stepped briskly to the speaker's stand.

"Gentlemen," he began, "we all know that each atom of matter is made up of a nucleus (of positive and negative electrons), with a certain number of negative electrons circling in orbits about it."

With this start, Deane rapidly and yet in detail began to sketch the well-known electronic theory of the constitution of matter. He glanced down at old walrus-face Cairns. The dark young girl smiled back encouragingly.

Deane continued, "The position of an element in the periodic table depends upon how many orbital electrons it has. Its atomic weight depends upon the number of its protons. Thus—"

"Just one moment!" interrupted a hoarse voice.

Deane abruptly stopped his address. The audience shifted uneasily in their seats, as they turned to face the interrupter. The walrus-like form of Professor Cairns lumbered heavily to its feet, and held up one flipper to command silence.

Silence was immediately forthcoming—silence tense and expectant. Deane flushed, ran his fingers through his tousled blond hair, and awaited the outburst from his professional rival. It came.

"Mr. President," bellowed Cairns, "can't this *young*" [emphasis on the "young"] "gentleman please assume that the members of this learned Society understand *some* of the principles of elementary chemistry?"

A titter began to run through the audience, but Deane strode to the front of the platform with flashing gray eyes, and silenced the titter with: "Not for one moment, Professor! I made *that* mistake the last time that I debated with *you*."

Then the titter broke forth again, and developed into a real laugh. Cairns slumped back into his seat, and puffed and snorted through his drooping moustache.

Charles Deane straightened, and swept the auditorium with a triumphant glance—and was immediately sorry for his wisecrack. True, it had silenced old walrus-face; but the girl, seated beside Professor Cairns, was staring up at him with an expression of mingled reproach and contempt.

Deane's face fell for an instant, then he shrugged his shoulders, and launched once more into his address. He explained the well-known periodic table of Moseley, which had enabled physicists to prophesy the characteristics of even the missing elements, a prophecy which had been justified and verified in every case.

DOWN IN THE audience, Professor Cairns started to rise again; then appeared to think better of it, and subsided. The dark slim girl beside him patted his arm.

Deane continued, "With the periodic table filled, from element 1 through element 92, it seemed impossible that there could exist any further substances in the universe. It never occurred to anyone that there might be an element numbered *zero*. Yet such an element is neuton, discovered by Harkins in 1933."

He paused dramatically, and smiled disarmingly; then went on: "Gentlemen, has it ever occurred to you that there may exist a whole new series of elements—elements numbered *minus* one, *minus* two, *minus* three, and so on— elements lighter by far than even hydrogen and neuton?"

There were some gasps and much glancing from one to another in the audience. And then a man in the front row asked incredulously, "But, Mr. Deane"—very few of the members of the Chemical Society could bring themselves to address their youngest colleague as *Doctor* Deane— "But, Mr. Deane, hydrogen and neuton each has an atomic weight of unity, by virtue of having only one proton. How is it possible for an atom to have less than *one* proton?"

From further back in the room, Professor Cairns bellowed sarcastically, "It might have *no* protons!"

"Exactly!" Deane replied. "It might have a *negative* nucleus, and thus weigh only 1/1845 as much as hydrogen!" *

---

* An atom of hydrogen consists of a positive nucleus, and one orbital negative electron. An electron weighs only about one 1836th of the weight of a proton. The atom of each element of the negative series has a negative nucleus, and orbital positive electrons one 1836th the weight of a negative electron, and hence one 3,000,000th the weight of a proton—utterly negligible. Element minus one weighs only one 918th as much as hydrogen, which formerly was supposed to be the lightest possible substance. Stratium has 8 nuclear negative electrons, 4 nuclear positive subelectrons, and 4 orbital positive subelectrons. Therefore it occupies position number minus four in the periodic table, belongs to the beryllium group of metals, and weighs only one 230th as much as hydrogen. It combines with hydrogen in much the way that plus members of the beryllium group combine with oxygen.

The first member of the negative elements was discovered in the following manner. Curry, while studying the emanations of radium, succeeded in rendering the beta rays electrically neutral, but did not realize that this result was made possible by the fact that beta rays consist of ions of a new element, number minus one of the periodic table, isolated and named "curriunx" by Charles Deane.

Deane's next discovery, the one which is pertinent to this narrative, was that the supposed hydrogen of the stratosphere is really stratium-hydride, a gaseous ore of

He paused to let that thought sink in, and then continued, "Such a series of elements *does* exist."

Professor Cairns snorted. Incredulity was written large on the faces of most of the audience. Deane confronted them belligerently.

"Go ahead and sneer!" he shouted. "You sneered in 1912, when Moseley revised the periodic table. You sneered at Jon Andrei, when he proved that beta rays cannot be produced unless hydrogen is present. You sneered at Harkins, when he discovered element zero. You sneered at Curry, when he claimed to have neutralized the beta ray of radium. So go ahead and sneer at *me*, when I tell you that I have not only identified the Curry ray as being element *minus* one, but also have succeeded in isolating element *minus* four, which I have named *stratium*."

Professor Cairns curled his lower lip, and blew through his moustache.

"Prove it, you upstart!" he snorted.

"Fair enough," Deane suavely replied, having by now recovered his calm, after his momentary outburst. "Seeing is believing, so I have brought some samples of stratium with me. Here, Angus."

Turning to his assistant, seated on the platform behind him, Deane held out his hand for a small package. The audience watched him uneasily, as he laid it on the speaker's stand and began to unwrap it.

Grinning amusedly, he remarked, "Don't worry, gentlemen. This thing isn't a bomb."

Within the wrapping-paper, there was a pasteboard

---

a new super-light metal, which he named "stratium." This metal can be extracted electrolytically from liquefied stratospheric hydrogen.

box. Deane removed the cover, and took out a number of pairs of cylindrical metallic sticks about the size of stubs of pencils. Each pair was fastened together with two elastics. One stick of each pair was dull gray in color; the other, brightly silver with a slight yellow tinge.

Deane explained. "Each piece of stratium is tied to a piece of lead, so as to hold it down. You can unfasten them if you wish, but be very careful not to drop the stratium. We might not be able to get it again, if you did."

He handed the samples to the members in the front row of seats. These gentlemen gingerly took them. Some felt of them, some smelled of them, some tried to scratch them with thumb-nail or penknife. Those in the rear of the audience stood up and craned their necks.

And then one man undid the elastics which bound his piece of stratium and lead together, and attempted to weigh the stratium in the palm of his hand. But the little rod of silver-yellow metal left his hand and soared abruptly aloft. Straight upward toward the high ceiling of the lecture-room it rose with ever accelerating speed, until it clinked upon the ceiling and lay there quietly as though on a floor. Everyone stared upward in amazement.

"Don't say I didn't warn you," Deane dryly remarked. "Now we'll have to send for the janitor and a ladder, to pick that piece of metal down."

The meeting speedily resolved itself into groups, to examine the little samples. Deane left the platform, and moved from group to group. Everywhere that he went, he became the focus of a barrage of inquiries. Those questions which related to his theories as to the nature and atomic constitution of the new metal, he answered; but he persistently refused to reveal where or how he had obtained his specimens.

At last he came to a group in the midst of which old Cairns, with sample in hand, was holding forth.

"Young man," said the professor, as Deane drew near, "this is a very clever hoax; but I mean to get to the bottom of it. With your permission, I shall take this piece of 'stratium,' as you call it, back to my own laboratories, and—"

"I'm very sorry, sir," Deane levelly replied, "but those samples are not for public distribution quite yet."

Cairns's little pig-eyes twinkled malevolently in his bullet head, as he snorted, "Aha! So I've smoked you out, eh? So it is a *hoax,* eh? So you don't dare submit your precious metal and your precious theories to a test?" Deane squared his chest, and clenched his fists. His gray eyes blazed. But the dark young girl stepped between them.

"Father, please! Mr. Deane, please," she said.

"I'm sorry," said Deane contritely, relaxing.

Cairns too relaxed. "Meet my daughter Donna," said he.

Deane took the girl's hand in his.

"You know," said he, "ever since I first came onto the platform this evening, I've wondered who you were."

"Really?" she asked, gently disengaging her hand.

Deane colored. "Again I'll have to say, 'I'm sorry,'" said he.

"Are you?" she bantered.

Then someone from another group asked a question, and dragged Deane away.

Finally, when the young scientist had made the rounds of all the groups, he signalled President Huntington to announce that the meeting was at an end, and sent Angus Frazer around to collect the samples of stratium.

The old Scotsman reported that one piece was missing.

"Of course," somebody nearby suggested, "it's up there on the ceiling."

"One in addition to that," Frazer dryly stated.

Deane conferred with President Huntington, and then the latter announced, "Those little sticks of stratium cost hundreds of dollars apiece to produce, and yet they are commercially valueless.

"I can hardly believe that any member of the Chemical Society is either a thief, or would be so unethical as to take one of these samples home for private experiment without the consent of the discoverer. But, under the circumstances, I am forced to direct the police to lock the doors and search the members."

There was a stir in the crowd, as Professor Cairns stepped forward, his long drooping moustaches twitching, and bellowed out, "Sir, this is an outrage. I, for one, refuse to be searched!"

3

ANOTHER MURDER!

CHARLES DEANE, ANXIOUS not to cause an open break with his old antagonist, hastened to interpose, "I'm willing to take the personal word of Professor Cairns that he hasn't the missing piece of stratium."

"And I refuse to give my word!" bellowed the old man.

A hush fell over the crowd, until someone announced, "Well, seeing as Cairns admits that he has the missing sample, that lets the rest of us out of being searched."

"I admit nothing!" Cairns snorted. "I admit nothing! I deny nothing! And I refuse to be searched! Now, what are you going to do about that, young fellow?"

"Oh, father, please don't!" murmured Donna Cairns.

Feeling quite certain that Cairns *did* have the missing piece of stratium, Deane replied to his query by saying, in as controlled a voice as his suppressed rage would permit, "What I am going to do about it, sir, is to invite you to my laboratory any time at your convenience, to be the first person outside of Angus Frazer and myself, to witness the actual extraction of stratium from its ore."

"But, sirr," objected Frazer, "what about the missing piece of strratium, sirr?"

"It can *stay* missing," Deane curtly replied, "rather than

insult the members of this learned society. President Huntington, you can call off the police."

Donna Cairns gave him a friendly approving smile. And all the audience started for the exits of the lecture-hall. The janitor arrived with a tall step-ladder, and went up after the piece of lighter-than-air metal which lay on the ceiling. Charles Deane and his assistant began to pack-up the sticks of stratium and their companion sticks of lead.

And then suddenly Deane realized something which had been struggling for recognition, just below the level of his consciousness, ever since shortly after the samples of metal had been passed around. The realization was this: the strange haunting man, with the sinister, swarthy face, beady black eyes, hooked nose, and beard—the man whom Deane had grown to think of as "the face"—this man was no longer in the lecture-hall.

Could it be that, after all, old Cairns was *not* the person who had made away with the missing piece of stratium?

The meeting was over. Angus had taken the box of little metal samples back to the laboratory, and Deane, strangely disturbed and ill-at-ease, had gone for a long swinging walk through the spring night alone.

"What was the matter with him?" he wondered. The meeting had been a great success. He had won the sympathy and approval of the audience, in spite of the attempts of Professor Cairns to heckle him. He had met a very pretty and attractive girl.

True, he had lost one of his precious samples of stratium; but, after all, what did that matter? Stratium had no commercial value, and the expense to which he had been put to produce his twenty samples, would have been the same if he had originally produced the nineteen which now remained to him.

The night was beautiful and starlit and balmy. Why, then, his depression and his feeling of impending disaster? His thoughts turned to the black-bearded face which had peered in through his laboratory door, on the day of the Diggs murder, and again that afternoon, and which he had seen yet again at the lecture that evening. But why worry about a Svengali face?

Deane shook himself out of his revery and glanced around. For some time he had been walking aimlessly, absorbed in his gloomy, foreboding thoughts, paying no attention to his whereabouts. Where was he, anyhow?

Then he gave a start. For he found himself standing on the sidewalk in front of the brownstone house occupied by his professional rival, Professor Cairns. And, presumably by the same token, also occupied by Donna Cairns, the wistful-faced daughter of the old walrus.

Was it thoughts of Donna that had directed his footsteps hither? Or was it something else, something sinister?

The street was ill-lit. Haunting forms seemed, to his over-wrought imagination, to lurk in the shadows of the doorways.

Shuddering, and wrapping his topcoat about him, Deane hurried out of the street to the better-lighted avenue at its end. Then took the subway downtown to his apartment.

All the way, he had the sensation of being followed.

He slept fitfully; and, after an early breakfast, went to his laboratory. Again he had the sensation of being followed.

Angus had not yet arrived, so Deane himself unlocked and opened the door.

The place was in disorder! Last night, before leaving, he and his old Scotch assistant had picked up and neatened everything; but now the floor was littered with broken bottles, retorts and test-tubes. Work benches had been shoved around, and one bench was even overturned. It was evident that some sort of a fight or struggle had taken place here.

But what? But why?

Deane bit his lip and hesitated to look around, dreading what he might find. Then clenching his fists, he began a complete survey of the wrecked laboratory.

His thought was that someone had come there to steal the remaining nineteen pieces of stratium. That would indeed be a loss, for those precious samples had cost him much time and hundreds of dollars! But, if so, why the struggle? Who had been here to defend them? Angus?

But Angus would have phoned him and notified him, if anything like that had happened. Unless—unless. Suppose his faithful old Angus had been knocked out or even killed, while defending the stratium.

Yes, there in a corner under one of the benches lay a crumpled human body, with its black-coated back turned toward him. Deane's heart skipped a beat, then raced madly. He drew a long breath, ran his fingers through his sandy hair; then stepped slowly and precisely toward the body.

Hunched up as it was, it looked too short and stocky to be that of the dour old Scotsman. And yet who else could it be?

It was *not* Angus. But those little pig-eyes staring wide-

open at him in death! That bullet-head, those long, drooping moustaches, that pugnacious jaw!

What was the dead body of Professor Cairns doing in
Charles Deane's laboratory?

Quite evidently the man was dead, in fact had been dead
long enough to have passed through the stage of rigor
mortis and be limp again. The face and hands were cold
to the touch. The eyeballs had begun to shrink and wrin-
kle. The vest was saturated with already dried and clotted
blood, and from the left breast there protruded the handle
of one of Deane's own laboratory knives!

This knife, the young scientist was very careful not to
touch. If someone planted this body here for the purpose
of framing him, he was determined to lend the scheme no
assistance in the form of finger-prints. True, they might be
old prints of his on the knife-handle, but these were by now
undoubtedly overlaid by finger-prints of the real assassin;
or, even if the assassins had worn gloves, the gloves must
have wiped off at least part of any old prints.

Then Deane's mind flashed back to the samples of stratium. So, putting on a pair of laboratory gloves, he gingerly
twirled the dial of his safe, and swung open the door. The
box of samples was *not* inside!

Next, to notify the police. But, as he moved toward the
telephone, it rang. Mechanically he picked up the cradle-
phone and said, "Charles Deane speaking."

An attractive and ingratiating male voice, totally strange,
replied, "Dr. Deane, are you in trouble?"

"Why—why—" stammered Deane. "Ah," said the voice,
"I can see that you are in trouble. Now—"

"But who are you?"

"I am a friend. Or, perhaps we had better say, an unknown admirer of your scientific achievements. You were about to telephone the police? Do not do so, I beg of you."

"But why not? And how do you know what I was going to do? And who are you, anyhow?"

"Isn't what you have found in your laboratory enough of a mystery, Dr. Deane, without your accusing me of being mysterious? But time is precious, so I want to tell you a few things about yourself. Listen."

"Yes."

"Then, in the first place, your assistant took the samples of stratium home with him. They are still safe. Last night, after your lecture, you had an unpleasant row with Professor Cairns, and went straight to his home. In spite of the lateness of the hour, you called him out."

"I did no such thing!" Deane indignantly exploded.

"Ah, but can you prove that you didn't?" the voice suavely inquired.

"No—. But—. I suppose not."

"All right, then," the voice continued. "We shall have to assume that you did. At any rate, Cairns' butler will testify that *someone* called for Cairns; and you can't deny that you were in the vicinity of his house at a late hour last night. So, to resume. You demanded that he come to your laboratory at once, to permit you to demonstrate your new discovery to him. 'Words followed,' as they say in stories. You lost your temper. And the rest you know."

"BUT I TELL you—" Deane indignantly began.

"Tell it to the Judge!" sternly snapped the voice.

"My God! Do you think—?"

"I *know!* Now listen to me, Deane. The case against you

An arm passed across his throat, throttling him

is perfect. You'll burn for the murder of Oscar Cairns. You need two things, and you need them in a hurry. First, some friend with influence and money, to hire one of the best detective firms in the country, to go after evidence, to prove that you are innocent. Secondly, some place to hide, while this evidence is being gathered."

"But I tell you I'm innocent!" Deane exclaimed. "The father of Donna Cairns is the last person in the world whom I would want to kill!"

"Oh, so that's how the land lies," said the voice; and there was a new note in it, which Deane couldn't quite make out. "Um! Well, do you wish me to help you? As I've already stated, the case against you is perfect."

"But why not surrender myself to the authorities, and let the District Attorney dig up the facts?" asked Deane, beginning to weaken.

"The most asinine thing you could possibly do!" the voice scornfully replied. "Did you ever hear of a prosecuting officer helping to prove anyone *innocent*. Come on! My time is valuable!"

Footsteps sounded in the corridor outside. Deane held his breath, but the footsteps continued on, past his door. He glanced at the dead body.

"All right! All right!" he yielded. "What do you wish me to do?"

"That's better," asserted the voice in a self-satisfied tone. "There's a taxi waiting for you at the front entrance to this building. Get into it and say nothing. The driver knows where to take you. Believe me, it's the only safe move for you. And you'd better hurry, for Angus Frazer will be here soon now, and then it'll be too late."

"All right. I'm coming," said Deane.

Returning the phone to its cradle, he gave one more look at the body of Cairns, more walrus-like in death even than in life; and then hurried out of the laboratory, and locked the door. He still had on his hat and topcoat.

He rang for the elevator. It came. He got in.

At the floor below, it stopped again. And there entered "the face," the man with the beady eyes, hooked nose, swarthy skin, and black beard. So this man had an office in the building? Or at least was addicted to snooping around other floors than Deane's.

"Nice day, sir, isn't it?" said the young chemist.

But the other, without moving his head, merely shifted his eyes to Deane's face and then looked away again, without reply.

At the street level, as soon as the elevator doors were opened, the man scuttled out and away; but Deane remained behind for an instant.

"Who's that?" he asked of the operator.

"A Mr. Smith. Office on the sixth floor. Moved in a little over a month ago."

"Hmp!" said Deane to himself. "So 'the face' isn't a snooper, after all. Well, I've got something real to worry about now, for a change."

So, with leaden steps, he made for the street.

There, sure enough, was a taxi. As Deane approached, the driver got out and opened the door.

THIS WAS UNUSUAL, for a taxi-driver usually merely reaches back from his seat to open the door for a patron. And the unusualness of the action registered itself even on Deane's perplexed and sorely tried brain. He even noticed that the driver's face was hollow-cheeked and pale.

How totally absurd it was for him to be getting into a cab with destination unknown, a cab obviously planted here by the real perpetrators of the murder of Professor Cairns! So Deane stopped abruptly, and did not get into the cab.

A slight noise to the left attracted his attention. He turned and saw the black-bearded, hunched-up "Mr. Smith," who had ridden down the elevator with him, now standing on the curb about twenty feet away, grinning at him with an uninterpretable expression.

Deane raised his hand to his head in perplexity, and the next instant he was seized by the scruff of the neck and the seat of the pants by the chauffeur, and was hurled through the open cab door into the dark interior of the cab.

His football training enabled him to land catlike, and to wheel almost as he landed. Then he gave a crouching spring at the closing door of the cab.

But the spring was never completed, for from behind him an arm passed across the front of his throat, throttling him and pulling him over backwards back into the cab.

Resourceful, his mind perfectly clear by now, he swung his right fist over his shoulder, and felt it strike a face. The grip upon his throat loosened, and he twisted around to confront his antagonist. The cab door clanged shut, and the cab started.

As the cab drove off, he heard a voice from the curb saying, "Good luck. Dr. Deane." And it was the same voice which he had heard over the phone.

Deane and the man with whom he was struggling, fell back against the seat, and instantly another arm was flung around Deane's neck. There were *two* men in the cab with him!

Shoving back his right elbow at the man who held him, Deane at the same time threw his left fist into a burly mustached face in front of him. The man in front of him collapsed, and Deane wheeled to confront the man behind. But this man, leaning back in the corner of the seat, caught Deane in the chest with his foot, and shoved the young chemist into the opposite front corner of the cab.

THEN THE TWO of them went at each other, with all four fists, as the cab bounded and jounced along.

Deane was just getting decidedly the better of the encounter, when the unconscious man on the floor came to, grabbed Deane's legs, and pulled him down. Then joined the mêlée.

The two thugs were more than a match for even an ex-football star. Gradually he began to weaken under their blows. Then a muffled shot rang out in the dark interior of the cab, and Deane's nostrils sensed the acrid stench of powder.

"You fool!" panted one of the men. "Lay off the gat! You know what Al—"

"Fool, yourself, for mentioning names," panted the other. "I'll shoot if I—"

The fist of the first speaker sent the gun flying, and Deane, taking advantage of this momentary diversion, pulled himself together for one last frantic effort, and knocked both of his captors cold. Deane took a good look at his two ex-captors. One had a swarthy Sicilian face with large moustache. The other, a bullet head with scarred jaw.

The cab had come to a stop beside the curb. Deane flung open the door and lurched out onto the sidewalk.

"Here you are, sir," said the taxi-driver genially, as though nothing had happened. "Right at the top of those steps. They'll be expecting you."

Deane gave his head a shake, to clear the cobwebs from his brain, and passed one hand through his hatless hair. Then stepped toward the cab to retrieve his hat; thought better of it, and stepped away again.

He looked past the cab, and across the street to the broad expanse of the Hudson.

"Riverside Drive," he said to himself.

He looked up at the house, at which the cab had deposited him. An impressive brownstone front. He glanced along the sidewalk in one direction, and there stood a policeman.

Deane took one step toward the cop, and opened his mouth to speak. Then suddenly realized that *he* had more to fear from the authorities than did his abductors.

The policeman by this time had evidently made up his mind to investigate, for he started to walk toward Deane. The taxi drove off. This left but one course open. Deane staggered up the steps of the brownstone house, and pushed the bell.

The policeman came to the foot of the steps, and stood there expectantly. The door opened, and a pompous butler stared in amazement at the bloody, disheveled figure which confronted him.

With every show of assurance, and in a tone loud enough to carry to the waiting policeman, Deane said, "Oh, it's all right, Higgins. Just a little tussle at the Club, that's all."

Then he forced his way past the butler, and closed the door behind him. The butler nearly exploded with outraged dignity and suppressed protest.

"But! But!" he spluttered.

"Higgins," said Deane levelly, "will you please tell your master that I've come. I understand that he is expecting me."

"Me nyme is *not* 'Iggins," pompously retorted the butler, "and your barging in 'ere in this wye is most irregular. 'Oo shall I sye, sir?"

"Dr. Charles Deane," the young scientist replied. "And I have already told you that your master is expecting me."

"Werry well, sir. Won't you set down, sir?"

And the butler moved off aggrievedly through a pair of high carved wooden doors, which he closed behind him.

THE HALLWAY WAS tall and somber. Deane stepped to a combined mirror, hatrack and umbrella stand, which stood along one wall; smoothed his hair and clothes, and cleaned the blood off his face with a wet corner of his handkerchief.

A sudden urge to flee swept through him. He seized the handle of the door. Then thought of the policeman outside, and stepped back again.

To himself he said, "I might as well be hung for a sheep as a lamb."

But somehow the word "hung" didn't sit so well, after what he had found under the bench in his laboratory.

Grimly he revised his quotation to, "I might as well be *electrocuted* for a sheep as a lamb."

Laughing harshly, he turned, just as the carved oak doors swung open again.

A man of uncertain age stepped out, erect and tailor-clad.

"Well, well," said he, extending his hand in friendly greeting. "This is indeed an honor, Dr. Deane. What brings you here? Busby told me that you seemed to be a bit battered up."

"Two thugs in a taxi-cab brought me here. They said that you would be expecting me."

Deane had uttered the first thoughts that came into his head, for his attention was riveted upon studying the face of his host. Where had he seen those suave clear-cut bronzed features before?

Suddenly it dawned upon him. He had seen that face in the newspapers and magazines. This was John Cortlandt Maitland, financial rival of Deane's late patron, Wolf Diggs.

Meanwhile Maitlandt was saying, "I don't know what you are talking about, Dr. Deane, for your visit here is a total surprise to me."

4

A GUEST OF THE MIGHTY

CHARLES DEANE WAS completely taken aback by Maitland's expressed ignorance of the object of his visit. Had the voice over the phone merely been playing a practical joke on him? But it must have been more than a mere joke, for the taxi-driver had brought him to a definite address, and the two thugs in the cab had certainly been in deadly earnest.

Deane stared into Maitland's face, and saw there merely an intensely friendly interest, slightly amused. But Deane's scientific training led him to register a resolve to keep his eyes open.

"Well," Maitland was saying, smiling, "regardless who sent you here, and regardless why he did it, it was certainly a favor to me, and I hope that it will turn out to have been a favor to you. Step into my library, and I'll ring for a drink. You look a bit shaken up. Which do you prefer, scotch or rye?"

"Neither," said Deane.

"Bourbon?"

"I don't drink, sir."

"Um," approvingly. "Neither do I. But I keep it on hand for guests."

Meanwhile Maitland was leading the way through the high carved oak doors into a room with book-lined walls, a massive table, and several red leather easy chairs and a couch. He sat down, and motioned to Deane to be seated.

Then, placing the tips of his slender fingers together, and staring quizzically at his guest through narrowed lids, he continued, "I'm glad you've come. Your visit here is a most fortunate coincidence, for I have admired your work in chemistry, and have regretted that you were not *my* protégé instead of being under the wing of my friend Diggs. So, when I learned of his sad death a month ago, I very nearly sent for you. But I kept putting it off, for fear that some mistaken sense of loyalty to your old employer might lead you to reject an offer of financial assistance from me. And here you are, of your own free will and accord. What a coincidence!"

"I'm hardly here of my own accord," laughed Deane. "And yet I'm certainly glad to have met you, if you can forgive the unconventional way in which it has happened."

"Yes, it certainly was unconventional," Maitland admitted, pursing up his lips and nodding his head several times. Then, "Have you any idea who the thugs were, and why they brought you to my house?"

"Well—yes," Deane reluctantly admitted.

Maitland watched him narrowly, with just the trace of an amused smile. Then said, "I want to be your friend, Deane. You are in trouble—serious trouble. I can tell it from your face. Perhaps you are even a fugitive from justice."

Deane's body jerked erect. So Maitland did know!

"Ah," continued Maitland, "I must have hit closer than I guessed. Well, you are safe from pursuit, so long as you remain in this house. I need your services in some chemical experimentation which I am about to undertake. Suppose we strike a bargain. Stay here as my guest and protégé."

"The fact that I have no other choice," said Deane levelly, "doesn't alter the fact that it will be a pleasure."

"Well spoken!" his host exclaimed. "You know, young many, I've taken an instinctive liking to you. And now suppose you unburden all your troubles. I am sure that I can help you. I've turned my hand to almost everything except detection of crime, and nearly always with success. Yes, I'm reasonably sure that I can help you."

So, almost before he knew it, Deane had plunged into an account of the happenings of the evening before. Why not? It would all be in the papers within a few hours. If Maitland were on the level, Deane ought to tell him everything; and, if Maitland were *not* on the level, he probably knew everything already. So Deane even mentioned the mysterious hunched figure, with the black beard. He told of his run-in with Professor Cairns, the loss of one of the samples of stratium, his walk past Cairns's house, his sensation of being followed, his grisly find in the laboratory this morning, the mysterious telephone call, the reappearance of the man with the beard, and the forced ride in the taxi.

But somehow he omitted to say anything about the bloody handkerchief which he had attempted to analyze. Probably it was his professional pride which kept him quiet; he did not like to admit that any chemical experiment had completely stumped him.

THROUGHOUT THE NARRATIVE, Maitland was suavity personified; but, though his mouth was smiling, his brown eyes were narrow slits, as he stared intently into the face of his guest.

Deane finished the account, and added, "What do you think of it, Mr. Maitland?"

Charles Deane

"I think that you are in a tough spot," was the answer. "The first thing that you need is a good lawyer." He pushed a desk-button, and as the butler entered, said, "Busby, get me Peter Markham at once."

Then, as the butler withdrew, Maitland continued. "The next thing that you need is the service of a detective agency, to dig up all the possible clues in your favor, before the District Attorney finds and suppresses them. Markham can arrange that detail for us. Then you need a new name, while you stay in my house. Servants might talk, you know. Except Busby; he's a regular clam. So, for the present, you'll be Mr. Horace Jones. You'll live in this house, and work in my basement laboratory."

Again he pushed the button, and this time told the butler, "Busby, show Mr. Jones to the second guest suite." Then to Deane, "Lunch is at one o'clock, Jones. Better rest in your room until then."

In the guest suite to which the butler showed him,

Deane sat heavily down upon the bed, and with elbows on knees, ran both hands through his tousled hair. What was it all about?

But gradually the calm, the orderliness, the seclusion of this household reassured him; so much so, that when Busby returned with morning papers and the morning editions of the evening papers, Deane was able to read, with aloof abstraction, the accounts of last evening's meeting and of the finding of Cairns's body. He was even able to smile a bit grimly at the realization that, if it had not been for the murder of Professor Cairns, the discovery of the new element stratium would not have been given one tenth of the space now accorded to it.

The newspaper accounts consisted largely of what Deane already knew; but, surprisingly, there was no mention of Angus Frazer. Also there were two additional items of importance. First, the night janitor had carried up in the freight elevator around midnight a large pasteboard carton marked "CHEMICALS. HANDLE WITH CARE," accompanied by Dr. Charles Deane, whom he well knew, and a short stocky gentleman who answered the description of the now deceased Professor Cairns. Neither had been seen to leave. Secondly, none of the day elevator-men could say for sure whether he had carried Dr. Deane up, but one of them distinctly remembered bringing him down, shortly after nine, this being impressed upon his mind by the fact that Dr. Deane had stopped and asked him the name of one of the other tenants of the building. Dr. Deane, so this elevator man said, had appeared excited and a bit bewildered, as though he had been drinking.

"Of all the rot!" exploded Deane, referring not to the part

about his having been excited and bewildered, which was undeniable, but rather to the part about his having gone up in the freight elevator with the deceased.

Just then the butler knocked again, this time with a suit, shirt, etc.

"Shall I draw your bawth, Mr. Jones?" he inquired solicitously.

"Thank you, yes, Busby," Deane replied, and began to undress.

The cuffs of his shirt were bloody and still damp, and as he stripped it off he noticed a peculiar and reminiscent smell. Hydrogen peroxide! The blood spots were drying, and some of them had begun to turn quite brown. Yet others were still a bright crimson. He sniffed of *them*. Yes, they were the source of the peculiar odor.

Some of the blood was not his own. Some of it was that peculiar substance which he had found on the handkerchief dropped by the bearded face, and which even his chemical skill had been unable to analyze!

ALTHOUGH THE BATH made him feel a lot better, it did not solve any of his perplexities. After dressing in the new clothes, which fitted him surprisingly well, Deane sat by the window, staring off across the Hudson, and trying to piece together the kaleidoscopic events of the last two days. But it was no use; the events refused to piece. He was sure that Maitland fitted somewhere into the picture; but just where?

He was still gloomily cogitating, when Busby knocked to announce luncheon. When descending to the main floor hall, Deane found all doors closed; and so, after a moment's hesitation, he opened the door which led into the study or library of his host. This would be a good place to wait for further instructions.

The room seemed to be empty, so Deane entered and closed the door. Then looked around. But the room was not empty. For on a red leather davenport in one corner behind the desk, lay Maitland on his hack, with mouth open, apparently asleep.

Deane was about to withdraw, when something about Maitland's appearance stayed him. The body seemed to be unnaturally motionless, the bronzed features seemed to be a shade paler than before, one hand and arm hung down limp over the edge of the couch, and there was no rhythmic rise and fall of the chest.

Tiptoeing, he knew not why, across the room, Deane leaned over the prostrate form, and listened. There could be no doubt now. There was no breath. Maitland was not breathing.

In one stride Deane reached the desk and pushed the button for the butler; then rushed back to the motionless body, snatched up the pendent hand, and searched for the pulse with trembling fingers.

He found the pulse; the heart was still beating, faintly. More than faintly; for as he shifted his fingers and slightly relaxed their frantic grip, he felt the pulse beat strong and full. Then the wrist was snatched from his grasp, and Maitland sat suddenly erect, brushing Deane aside and nearly upsetting him.

AS DEANE STAGGERED back, both from the impact and from surprise, Maitland shook his head, blinked, and then stared fixedly at Deane.

"Young man," said he sternly, "you gave me quite a scare. Just what was the idea of disturbing me when I was asleep?"

Deane laughed embarrassedly.

"I'm sorry, sir," he apologetically replied, "but *you* gave *me* a scare, too. I thought you were dead. You didn't seem to be breathing."

At these words, Maitland's head jerked around, and his eyes narrowed to slits.

"Young man," said he, and there was menace in his tone. "Don't you ever again, while you are my guest, meddle in anything which does not concern you."

Deane was about to stammer some apology, when the door opened, and the butler entered, saying, "You rang, sir?"

"It was an accident, Busby," Maitland replied.

"Werry well, sir. But I was about to announce luncheon, anyway, sir."

Maitland smiled up at Deane, all trace of his recent tense resentment gone. Then rising, he said jovially, "Well, let's eat." And led the way across the room, down to the hall, and through another door, into a dining room. Deane too by this time had recovered his outward calm, but inwardly his scientifically trained mind was searching for a solution of his host's strange behavior.

Two other persons were already at table: a beautiful, statuesque blonde of about twenty, with black eyebrows; and a small fat pudgy man of middle age, with white grub-like fingers and very dirty nails.

As they entered, the man arose.

"Mavis, dear," announced Maitland, indicating Deane with a gracious wave of his hand, "this is Mr. Horace Jones, who will stay with us for a while as a member of the family, and assist me with some chemical experimentation. Mr. Jones, my daughter Mavis. And this is my good friend and legal counselor, Peter Markham."

Miss Maitland raised her black eyebrows, incredulously, as she said, "So you're to help father with his chemistry? Welcome to our midst."

"I've heard about your scientific work, Mr.—Jones," added the lawyer.

Maitland's brows contracted slightly, as his dark eyes flashed a quick signal of disapprobation to each of the two speakers.

Then with his old suavity he indicated a chair to his guest, and took his own place at the head of the carved oak table.

Her yellow green eyes half closed, and her face expressionless, Mavis Maitland leaned toward Deane and purred, "And now tell me all about yourself, Mr. Jones. You say you come from Boston?"

"I didn't say," laughed Deane a bit uneasily. "But, as a matter of fact, I was born and brought up right here in your old New York."

Maitland, jerked his head around toward his guest, without change of expression, and then turned toward the pudgy little lawyer again. The warning was clearly and unmistakably understood by Deane.

Meanwhile Maitland's daughter was saying abstractedly, "Really? How very interesting."

THROUGHOUT THE MEAL which followed, Maitland and Markham discoursed together, in an undertone, of cases and deals. Once Deane pricked up his ears as he thought he heard the words "heavy water," but the conversation did not seem to refer to chemistry. From time to time, Maitland's daughter would ask Deane some question about himself, and then appear to doze off while watching him through half-closed sleepy cat-like eyes as he answered.

After the dessert, Mavis excused herself; and, over the coffee and cigarettes, the conversation turned to Deane's predicament.

"Mr. Jones," said lawyer Markham, with a briskness which his pudginess belied, "I shall continue to address you as 'Mr. Jones' just for practice, although of course I know your true identity. In the few hours since Mr. Maitland put me in charge of your case, I have been able to learn much through undercover methods. And there is one item which is rather disquieting."

"By the way," Deane interrupted, "have you learned anything of my old assistant, Angus Frazer? The newspapers don't mention him; and I haven't heard from him or about him since we left the lecture together last night."

How long ago that seemed!

"You have heard nothing since then?" asked Maitland pointedly.

Deane shifted uneasily.

"Well," he admitted, "the voice which talked over the phone to me in the laboratory early this morning told me that Angus had gotten home safely with the samples of stratium."

"Do you know anything of this Frazer?" Maitland asked of Markham.

The little lawyer shrugged his shoulders and spread out his dirty-tipped fingers.

"Such a business!" he complained. "Well, my real information can wait, I suppose. Yes, I *do* know about Frazer."

"Yes?" asked Deane, leaning forward eagerly.

The little lawyer sniffed.

"He's locked up in the Tombs," he announced laconically.

"What on earth for?" exclaimed Deane indignantly.

"For supposed complicity in two murders!"

"Two?"

"Yes, two. And you're wanted for both, Charles Deane. Your finger prints were found; on the gum which shot the Wolf of Wall Street, as well as on the knife which stabbed Professor Cairns."

Maitland was watching his protégé intently through narrowed lids, as the fat little lawyer made this announcement.

"Why, I never touched the thing!" Deane indignantly exclaimed. "And I took pains that no one else should touch it, either."

"How very unfortunate," said Markham, wagging his head. "For, if someone else had touched it, they might have smeared, your finger prints. As it is—"

"But how could anyone know my prints? I've never been finger-printed."

"Oh, they found plenty of those all over everything in your laboratory."

"It looked to me, Mr. Deane—" Maitland levelly began.

"Jones, sir," Markham reminded him.

"Don't interrupt," Maitland snapped. "It looks to me, Mr. Deane, as though you were unquestionably guilty of both murders."

"But, Mr. Maitland," Deane objected, turning a hurt and surprised face toward his employer, "I tell you that—"

Maitland held up his hand with a suave smile.

"Oh," said he, "I don't say that you had anything to do with either killing, but yet I do say that you are guilty of both. Being guilty does not depend on facts; it depends on the evidence. And the evidence is overwhelmingly against you. I am afraid that I can't keep you here any longer."

5

FLIGHT

"VERY WELL," SAID Deane, getting up from the table a bit unsteadily. "Somehow this haven seemed too good to be true. But why did you play with me, Mr. Maitland? Why did you tell me that you would protect me, and then leave me in the lurch? Why not turn me over to the police, and be done with it?"

"My dear young man," Maitland exclaimed, jumping up and placing one hand on Deane's shoulder. "You have sadly misunderstood me. When I said that I could no longer keep you here, I meant that I must take you to some safer place. I have a hunting lodge in the Black Hills, where no one would ever think of looking for you. We shall, start for there tonight. What do you think, Peter?"

"I think it would be a most excellent idea," said Markham obsequiously.

"Forgive me for having doubted you," said Deane gratefully, and yet not altogether convinced, as he sat down again.

"It's all decided then," said Maitland briskly. "We start tonight in my plane."

"But what about good old Angus?" Deane objected.

"I hate to leave him behind. Can't you do something for him, too?"

Maitland smiled coldly. "That's a big order," he said casually, "but I'll see what can be done about it. And now, will you please step into my library, and amuse yourself with whatever books and magazines you can find, while I arrange the trip."

It was a dull afternoon for the young scientist. In spite of the excellent chemical library of his host, his mind kept dwelling on his predicament.

He could not fathom the mystery of how his fingerprints came to be on the gun which he had taken such pains not to touch. Doubtless they had been planted there by the same persons who had planted Professor Cairns's body in Deane's laboratory. But who could these persons be, and what was their object in attempting to pin these two crimes onto him?

And this man Maitland! Deane did not know quite what to make of him. He was an affable, genial, considerate host; and certainly was protecting Deane from the police. And yet he had a coldly calculating inscrutability, which baffled his young protégé. What was his motive anyway? For obviously a man of his Wall Street reputation wasn't out of mere kindness protecting a total stranger wanted for two murders.

And Maitland's daughter Mavis! Resembling her father in many respects; and, like him, inscrutable. But her inscrutability had a feline touch which was most intriguing.

Many times in that long afternoon, Deane characteristically ran his fingers through his sandy hair, and shook his head in bewilderment. His scientifically trained mind told him that something was wrong. But what? He could only watch and wait.

Finally he became interested in a collection of pamphlets and magazine articles on heavy water, articles by Rutherford and Oliphant and Harteck, articles on how these three scientists had discovered deuterium and triplogen, articles speculating on the place which heavy water might play in the drama of life and death.

Deane read all this material with a purpose, for anything in which Maitland was sufficiently interested to invest thousands of dollars, might throw some light on the mystery of his character. But, as he read on, Deane soon forgot all about his host, and became absorbed in pure scientific interest.

Dinner was served to him alone in the library, and quite early. Then Busby brought him a hat and overcoat and gloves, and apologetically announced, "The master says as 'ow you 'ad better put on this false mustache. In case anyone might recognize you, sir."

So saying, Busby handed over a dark mustache, a small mirror, and a bottle of collodion. And, feeling very foolish and melodramatic, Deane put it on.

It completely changed his appearance, especially when his cap and overcoat-collar covered his blond hair.

Then Maitland and his daughter joined him. There was a twinkle in the banker's eye as he inspected the mustache, and Mavis gaily laughed aloud. But they hurried out to the car, before Deane had time to become embarrassed.

Mavis sat between the two men in the rear seat of the car. Leaning a little toward Deane, she smiled up at him and said, "Have you flown much, Mr. Jones? I just adore it. I am a licensed pilot and drive my own plane." No longer sleepily feline, she seemed tense and vibrant. Deane marveled at the change in her, as she chattered on, all the way to the flying field.

Maitland sat stiffly erect, staring straight ahead with half-closed eyes, immersed in thought.

AT THE NEWARK airport, their car was driven up to the side of a large tri-motored plane. As they alighted, another car drove up, and Peter Markham got out with a tall and rather bewildered looking gentleman with reddish sideburns, whom the pudgy little lawyer introduced as "Mr. Campbell."

"Vurra pleased to make your-r acquaintance," said Campbell.

A pang shot through Charles Deane. The voice, the manner, of this newcomer reminded him so poignantly of his old Scotch assistant, whom he was leaving behind in jail. But he was bustled aboard the plane, with but little chance for thought. He and Campbell sat together.

As the plane took off toward the West in the starlit night, Deane remarked, "You know, you remind me of a friend of mine."

Then bit his lip, as he realized that no hints at all as to his identity should be given out. Yet, unthinking, he removed his hat, thus uncovering his unruly sandy hair, in incongruous contrast to his black mustache.

"And you, too, sir-r," began the Scot; and then he too bit his tongue.

"Oh, by the way," remarked Maitland, ambling back to them, and leaning against the seat ahead. "You two ought to get really acquainted. Dr. Deane, meet Mr. Frazer."

"What!" exclaimed the two seat-mates, staring at each other.

"You can take off your disguises now," said Maitland, with a twinkle in his eye. "We know you."

"But how did Angus—" Deane began."

"Easy enough," Maitland explained. "Markham got a professional bondsman to put up bail for him, and here he is, skipping bail. That's all. And now I've got *two* chemists to work for me, instead of merely one."

He turned and went forward to the pilot's compartment, while Charles Deane and old Angus compared notes, and tried to piece together the events which had enmeshed them.

During most of the trip, Maitland stayed with the pilot. In fact, he drove the machine himself part of the way. Mavis kept to herself, reading or staring out of the window into the black night, until Deane tired of the company of his middle-aged laboratory assistant, and wished that she wouldn't. But she left him no opening for an approach. Natural diffidence kept him from making up to the elusive daughter of his employer.

After a while, the lights were turned off, and he curled up in his seat and slept.

AROUND NOON THE next day, the plane came down on a small landing-field surrounded by high mountains. Deane judged they must be somewhere in North Dakota. On the side of one foothill there stood a pretentious log-cabin overlooking the field. Thither Maitland led his guests.

"Welcome to Sioux Lodge," said he.

The main room of the lodge was lined with mounted heads and with stuffed fishes on plaques. Fur rugs were on the floor. At one end was a fireplace and a chimney of rough field stones, on which hung a framed motto, the one incongruous note amid all these surroundings.

The motto *had* read: "We can afford to wait." But all the words, except the last, had been crossed out by two brush strokes; above them was now scrawled the single word "Why"; and the period had been roughly changed to a question-mark, so that the motto now proclaimed: "Why wait?"

Maitland had gone to give directions to the servants. Angus Frazer was examining some of the specimens at the other end of the room. Deane stared at the motto with considerable puzzlement, and ran his fingers thoughtfully through his hair. Somehow he instinctively felt that this altered sentiment held the clue to many things. Somehow his mind flashed back to the time he had found Maitland lying unbreathing, apparently dead, in the latter's study in New York.

As he stared at the motto, and sought to fathom its mystery, a soft hand was laid on his arm, and the voice of Mavis Maitland spoke in his ear, "My friend, ask no questions about that sign."

Then wheeling him around to face her, she smiled up at him, and continued," I know that you don't like me, Mr. Deane—or rather, Mr. Jones, as you must be known for some time— But you might as well make up your mind to stand for me, for you are going to see quite a lot of me from now on."

Deane smiled back at her; but his thoughts were on the similarity between her warning, just given, and her father's warning at the time that Deane had awakened him from his unbreathing sleep.

Two months later. They had been busy months for Charles Deane and Angus, and the several hundred workmen whom Maitland had imported. In fact, Deane's work had been so preoccupying that he had practically given up speculating upon the peculiar circumstances attendant on his being here.

Several laboratories had been built on the mountainside. Into one of these Deane was never permitted to enter. Here Maitland spent a great deal of his time, assisted by two very taciturn individuals, one of whom Deane learned was a doctor, and the other one a chemist. This laboratory intrigued Deane greatly, especially when he happened to spot, on the label of a highly insured container bound for that building, the word "denterium" for somehow he had developed an intense interest in the subject of heavy water.

He asked Maitland to be allowed to help him, but was rebuffed in such a manner that he did not care to raise the question again.

In addition to the laboratories, there was a storehouse and a smelter. A huge balloon had carried one end of a small pipe up into the stratosphere, and, through this pipe the peculiar gases of that far height had been pumped down, and separated into their constituents. From the stratium-hydride gas, the rare element, stratium, was electrolytically extracted, and then sent to the smelters to be melted into bars.

Everything was paradoxical, contrary to nature!

Sinking a shaft into a blue sky, instead of into the ground, to mine for metallic ore! Extracting that ore from the mine in gaseous, rather than solid, form! Bringing the ore down, instead of up, to the surface of the earth!

But the smelter was even more absurd! Crucibles hanging upside down, with their open ends facing downward. Fires applied above them. Pieces of metal dropped up into them. Liquid metal boiling merrily at the bottom—or top, if you prefer to call it so—of inverted bowls; and finally being poured upward over the lip into moulds hanging above the crucibles.

And the storehouse was the most absurd of all! Gantry cranes running on rails low to the floor, with their traction-wheels bearing up against the bottom side of the rails. Chains hanging straight up into the air from the winches on the cranes, and holding down at their upper ends, huge bars of silver-yellow metal heavily striving to fall upward to the ceiling, where hundreds of similar bars lay piled, row on row. And, when the winch was slacked off, and the chains paid out, the bar would gradually rise, until the chain was finally cast off, and the bar clinked up, to rest on the bottom of one of the ceiling piles. Shipments of stratium from this storehouse were frequently sent out by trucks, destination unknown to him.

Charles Deane often shook his head over it all, and ran his fingers through his sandy hair.

THIS HUGE ESTABLISHMENT for stratosphere mining was far beyond anything of which he had dreamed when working in the little laboratory financed by Wolf Diggs. It was large-scale, stupendous, magnificent, characteristic of the personality of Deane's new patron, John Cortlandt Maitland.

And, like the establishment, Maitland was a paradox.

Just as Deane was never quite able to understand, to realize, this stratosphere mining venture, so also Maitland himself never appeared quite real, quite understandable. No further clues had turned up as to his motives.

And his daughter Mavis was no less inscrutable. Catlike and sleepy in the daytime, at night she emerged into something elfin and eerie. Often she and Deane walked together in the evening; and yet he felt that he did not know her at all, until one night—

Maitland's conversation at supper had taken one of its cryptic philosophical turns. "I shall never marry again," he had said, placing the tips of his slender fingers together, and surveying his auditors through narrowed lids. "Do you know why people marry? It is because of the craving for immortality. Racial immortality, since personal immortality is not available to most of us. In the words of the Persian poet Jami:

> " 'O, thou whose wisdom is the rule of kings—glory to God who
> gave it—answer me: is any blessing better than a son? Man's
> prime desire, by which his name and he shall live beyond himself.
> A foot for thee to stand on he shall be, a hand to stop thy falling.
> In his youth thou shalt be young, and in his strength be strong.'
> "And yet for some of us—"

He had paused abruptly, had looked up at the altered motto hanging above the fireplace, and had smiled a smile so peculiar that no one had cared to ask him to explain the riddle of his words.

And now, as Deane walked beside Mavis along a moonlit mountain trail, his thoughts flashed back to the strange words of her father; and he wondered.

But one could not walk with Mavis Maitland and keep his thoughts for long on anything other than Mavis. In white dress, with a pale green scarf thrown lightly about her shoulders, she looked like a slim white birch tree, slender and graceful and weird, yet with a cold strength within.

In a little clearing they paused, hand in hand, and stared out across the moonlit mists of the valleys. And then she turned and pressed softly against him, looking up at him with expressionless face, her yellow-green eyes veiled by long lashes beneath pencilled lines of black.

"Mavis," he breathed, and swept her into his arms.

For some minutes they stood thus. Then gently she disengaged herself. Her lips were tight, her pointed jaw firm, her eyes narrow slits. Slowly she shook her head.

"No," said she. "It cannot be. This is the penalty that I must pay. Of course, father could make you one of us. But if you were one of us, you would no longer be able to love. Father has said so. And if you were not one of us, our love would be too fleeting. And—"

"What on earth are you talking about?" Deane exclaimed, horrified.

"Nothing you would understand."

"But, Mavis—"

"No! No! And now will you please do me a favor?"

"Why, certainly—"

"I knew you would. And it is something very simple. Let me go home alone."

"But, Mavis—"

"You promised. And now kiss me again."

Once more he held her close. Then suddenly with a little cry of pain she disengaged herself.

"Your ring has cut my hand. See!" And she held it up for his inspection in the moonlight.

With a stammered apology, he mopped a tiny red scratch with his handkerchief. Then kissed her gently on the forehead, craving forgiveness.

HER EXPRESSION WAS now once more the sleepy cat of daytimes. But her rigid body and clenched hands belied the expression.

Then she fled from him down the moonlit mountainside path. And, true to his promise, Deane did not follow her. Instead, he stared longingly after the fleeing green-white figure, and reverently raised to his lips the handkerchief which had staunched her tiny wound.

Then dropped it with surprise.

For the familiar odor of hydrogen peroxide assailed his nostrils!

Sliding pebbles on the path behind him suddenly caused him to wheel about. Down the trail lurched a heavy squat figure, with round head and scraggy beard. Its arms flopped flipper-like as it walked.

As Deane turned to confront it, it paused irresolute as though to flee. Then, with a hopeless gesture, it fell forward. Deane jumped and caught it as it fell. Then eased the body gently to the ground.

A mountain stream flowed beside the path. Deane wet his handkerchief and bathed the face of the gnomelike man. Its eyes opened, small piglike eyes, and stared unseeingly up at him. Then focused, and studied him incredulously—and fearfully.

"Dr. Deane, eh?" asked a husky voice. "Then it really was you who kidnapped me."

"Yes, I'm Deane all right," he replied, forgetting for the moment the part which he had been playing. "But I didn't kidnap you, or anyone. Never saw you before in all my life. Who are you?"

The gnome smiled gruesomely through its unkempt beard.

"*You* ought to know, for you brought me here. But I suppose I have changed since then. Don't you recognize your old enemy Cairns? Professor Oscar Cairns? And now take me back to my jailers."

6

A PRISONER!

"**BUT YOU'RE DEAD!**" Deane exclaimed, looking down with horror at the unkempt bearded face which was staring up at him in the white moonlight. "I saw you lying dead on the floor of my own laboratory, back in New York. I'm wanted by the police, for murdering you. Though I didn't do it, I swear I didn't," he hastened to add.

"Naturally not!" snapped Professor Cairns, sitting suddenly erect, and frowning at the younger man.

Both men continued to stare at each other for several minutes in the moonlight, first incredulously, then reflectively, then quizzically, and finally with a broad grin, which broke into a laugh.

"Put it there, young fellow," bellowed Cairns, holding out one flipper. "Let's bury the hatchet. We're both in some sort of a fix; the same fix, if you'd ask me. Let's be scientific about this. Let's compare notes before my jailers catch up with me."

"Your jailers?" asked Deane, still incredulous. "What do you mean jailers?"

"I must be brief," declared the Professor, casting his little pig-eyes apprehensively first up and then down the moonlit mountain trail. "The night of your lecture on 'Stratium'—and, by the way, I did *not* steal that sample stick—when I got home from the lecture, I decided to stay up for a while, and read some articles by Moseley and Curry, to see if they might not throw some light on your alleged discovery."

Deane grimaced at the word "alleged."

Professor Cairns noticed the grimace—the moon was bright enough for that—and apologetically murmured, "My error. As the modern generation say, 'Skip it.' But, to get on. Quite awhile later, my butler announced that some gentlemen wanted to see me at the front door. I suppose that the strangeness of a call at that late hour ought to have impressed itself on me. But I was so engrossed with my reading that I didn't notice what time it was. I went to the door. And there you stood, between two rather rough-looking characters."

"I did not!" Deane hotly retorted. The Professor held up one flipper. His little pig-eyes twinkled.

"No, no, of course not," he deprecated. "I'm merely reporting what happened, as it appeared to me at the time."

"Just a minute," Deane interrupted, with the sudden flash of an idea in his eyes. "Was one of them a swarthy Sicilian with long bushy mustaches? And did the other have a round bulletlike head like a pugilist, with a scarred chin?"

"Why—yes."

"Go on."

"But why?"

"Go on!"

"Very well. You seemed agitated and urged me to get into a taxi which was standing at the curb. You said that you wanted me to go at once to your laboratory to witness a startling new development."

"Did you notice—"

"The driver? Yes. A face very sallow, and skull-like."

"Ah! Go on."

"That's about all. I don't even remember getting into the taxi. The next thing that I knew, I was in a plane, speeding through the night—"

"Just a minute," Deane interrupted. "Listen!"

Far up the moonlit trail could be heard the sound of voices. "It's they!" exclaimed the Professor in a hushed altered voice.

Deane needed no explanation of those words.

"Come on!" he whispered, pulling the older man to his feet. With sure steps, he led the way at right angles off the trail up the mountainside to the purple shadow of a clump of bushes, where the two men squatted down silently to wait.

THEY DID NOT have long to wait. To the accompaniment of sliding pebbles, the voices drew nearer. Grumbling voices. From behind the bush, the two fugitives could make out the black forms of three burly brutes, slipping and sliding down the trail.

Said one of the three jailers, "What do you suppose became of the old walrus? He was too weak from starving himself to get very far."

"I 'ope 'e fell orff a precipice, that I do," fervently grumbled one of the others.

"Here's his handkerchief," said the third, picking up the one which Deane had used to staunch Mavis's wound and to bathe the Professor's forehead.

"Come on!"

Then they passed on, down the trail.

Professor Cairns snorted softly.

"You were saying—" Deane suggested.

"Oh, yes. Where was I? Oh, yes. The airplane, in which I was a prisoner, flew all day, and well into the next night. We passed above small cities, and crossed rivers, but I was unable to recognize any of them. We seemed to be avoiding landmarks and large metropolises. Finally, late at night, we landed in these mountains. I was pushed and shoved up a trail—this trail, I think—and was locked up in a sort of cabin prison, which seems to be in charge of a handsome dark young fellow named Alpheus. He is in command of quite a number of low-brow thugs—you've just seen three samples of them—but Alpheus himself seems to be quite intelligent—educated even."

"But what was the great idea?" Deane exploded. "What did they want of you?"

"They desired my assistance in some chemical experiments, I believe," the old Professor dryly replied, "but I have consistently refused to work for them. No one can drive *me*."

DEANE SMILED TO himself at the thought of anyone trying to drive the pugnacious old man. Then sobered at the realization of how he himself had been duped. True, he had been suspicious of Maitland's motives right along; but it had never occurred to him to doubt that at least he was being afforded a hide-out from the police who wanted him for the murder of Oscar Cairns. And now to think that all this while Cairns himself had been living safe and sound within a couple of miles of him!

"Cairns," said he, with sudden realization, "this thing is bigger than we think. Maitland has never been known to do anything for any one other than Maitland, and never anything that wasn't on a grand, stupendous scale. His kidnapping of you, and his tricking Angus and me into coming here voluntarily, means something. Something not so good. Let's find out what it is, and stop it."

"Just a minute, young man," Cairns objected. "You forget that you haven't yet told me what *you* are doing here. You seem to be allied with my captors—and yet you just now helped me to escape from them. A few minutes ago you said something about being wanted for having murdered *me!* And just now you mentioned Maitland. Do you mean Maitland, the New York banker? What can *he* have to do with all this thuggery?"

"A plenty!" Deane exclaimed. "I'll tell you."

Then briefly, in that incongruous setting—the shadow of a bush on a moonlit North Dakota mountainside—the younger of the two scientists briefly sketched to the other the scrambled events that had occurred since the two of them had parted in anger at the meeting of the Chemical Society—long, long ago, it seemed—in old New York. As he recounted those events, they took on new meaning, by virtue of the disclosures of the present evening.

The death of Wolf Diggs in his Wall Street office, a death of which Deane had been accused because of finger-prints on a gun handle. But, now that Professor Cairns had been found alive, was it not possible that Diggs too was still among the living? Or, at least, that Deane was not wanted for this murder at all, and that the story of the finger-prints had been a mere invention of Maitland's greasy little lawyer, Markham?

The successful kidnapping of Cairns, and the unsuccessful attempt at kidnapping Deane—by the same taxi-driver and two thugs. Unsuccessful? How absurd! For both kidnappings had had the same result, namely, to deliver the victim into the hands of Maitland.

Although the technique had been different in each instance—and, too, in the capturing of Angus Frazer by the simple expedient of putting up his bail-money—nevertheless Maitland had in each instance "got his man."

Cairns naming his head jailer as Alpheus, and the thoughtless mention of "Al—" by one of the thugs in the taxi. Could these be the same?

Of course, Deane could not figure out any of the details. For example, who had impersonated him to Cairns, and whose body was it that he had found in his laboratory, etc., etc.? And then, too, there were certain other items, apparently unimportant in themselves, which intrigued him. Such, for example, as: who had stolen the little sample of stratium at the lecture, and why; why had Maitland apparently not been breathing that time asleep in his study; and what was the meaning of the alteration of that motto, hanging in Maitland's hunting lodge, from "We can afford to wait" to "Why wait?"

But, of course, the major question was: What was this all about, anyway? What was Maitland's racket? For Deane was by now absolutely convinced—what he had suspected ever since he himself had sought haven in Maitland's brownstone front on Riverside Drive—that Maitland was systematically working toward some gigantic and sinister scheme.

Thus Deane's thoughts wandered, as he sat on the moonlit mountainside, in the shadow of a bush with the old professor, and recounted the story of how he had become enmeshed in Maitland's web.

But there was one part of the story which he changed. He did not tell the professor the true reason why he happened to be on this trail at this time of night, for he felt that Cairns might mistrust him if the old man knew the extent of his intimacy with Maitland's daughter Mavis. So, instead, he merely stated that he had felt restless that evening, and had gone out for a walk.

Old Cairns thrust out his chin belligerently, and blew a blast of breath through one side of his unkempt mustaches. His little black eyes twinkled appreciatively. Weak and disheveled though he was, he was once more his old self again.

"So that's the situation, is it, eh?" he snorted, lumbering to his feet. "Come on! I'm going back."

"What on earth for?" exclaimed Deane, springing up too, and staring with puzzlement at the old professor in the moonlight.

"I'm going back," asserted Cairns resolutely, "for the purpose of seeming to give in to my captors. To the chemical work which they captured me for. To keep my eyes and ears open, and find out what it's all about. Come on!"

"Me?" Deane asked, bewildered.

"Certainly," the old professor asserted.

"But what will your captors—? Oh, I see," appreciatively. "I'll walk back with you, so as to make certain that you get there all right, and so as to learn the exact location of your cabin. My staying out an hour extra won't make any difference. I'm with you!" So the two of them set out up the trail together. And it was just as well that Deane came along, for the old professor—once his flare-up of energy and resolution was over—could never have made it alone.

Together they made it. Then, while Cairns sat and puffed in a chair in the prison cabin, Deane bustled around, brewed the old man some tea, and then put him to bed.

SOMEWHAT REVIVED, CAIRNS said, "And now, *auf wiedersehen*. I'll be all right by morning. And won't those thugs be surprised! And won't Alpheus accuse them of pipe-dreaming my escape. But as to *your* plans—what do you suggest?"

"Well—" Deane replied ruminatively, "now that I'm no longer chargeable with having killed you, and as that charge is all that Maitland is using to hold me here, why not have me escape from here, give myself up, and then tip off the authorities to watch and investigate Maitland, meanwhile keeping me locked up on the murder charge, so that Maitland won't suspect."

But Cairns shook his head. "No good!" he snorted contemptuously. "The authorities would never believe that I am alive. They might even blunder out here and show their hand, which would be worse.—I have it! I'll write a note to my daughter Donna. She knows young McGrady, the District Attorney! With her convinced and on your side, and you keeping under cover in my house, she ought to be able to line things up satisfactorily with the authorities. Have you a pencil and paper?"

Abstractedly, Deane reached in his pocket for an Ever-sharp and a little leather-clad notebook which he always carried. But his thoughts were far away in both time and space: back in old New York at the meeting of the Chemical Society, at which he had delivered his fateful paper on the new negative metal stratium. Oscar Cairns had been there, belligerently opposing him, doubting his epoch-making discovery of a metal hard as steel and lighter than air. And, sitting beside Cairns, had been a slim dark girl, with wavy brown hair and a wistful mouth, elfishly uptilted at the corners. Donna Cairns!

And then his thoughts abruptly shifted to the very different girl whom he had passionately held in his arms an hour ago. Mavis Maitland! Steel cold and mysterious.

Deane felt embarrassed and disloyal. Disloyal to the memory of Donna for having held Mavis in his arms. Disloyal to Mavis for now thinking so poignantly of Donna.

"Wake up, and snap out of it, young fellow," bellowed Cairns. "Here's the note to Donna, and you'd better be on your way before Alpheus and his thugs return. You and I are going to work this thing out. Goodby and good luck."

"Goodby, sir," said Deane, gripping the older man's hand. But his eyes were not on Cairns; instead he was looking beside the old professor, where in his imagination he saw the wistful face of Donna Cairns.

Then he blew out the light, stepped from the darkened cabin into the moonlit night, and strode resolutely down the trail toward the hunting-lodge and attendant buildings of the encampment of John Cortlandt Maitland.

As he strode along, with narrowed eyes and set jaw, he tried to focus his thoughts on the problem which he was about to tackle, but instead his mind kept wandering to the vision of two beautiful faces, one crowned with brown hair and the other crowned with an aureole of gold, one impishly wistful, and the other coldly glamorous.

The comparison was so intriguingly engrossing that Deane soon lost all realization of where he was. His feet automatically picked their way down the moonlit trail; but, apart from that, he was oblivious to his surroundings.

A CLOUD PASSED across the face of the moon, just as Deane rounded a turn in the path. The contrast of sudden darkness was sufficient to jar him out of his reverie. He halted abruptly, and glanced around to get his bearings.

And at the same instant, he heard sliding pebbles ahead, and a voice exclaiming, "Hi sye! Did you see wot Hi saw? The owld codger hisself."

"I saw it too," came the reply in a gruff voice slightly subdued and awed, "but it wasn't old Cairns. Too tall and slim."

Instantly alert, Charles Deane stepped quickly off the trail to one side, groping carefully with his feet so as to avoid setting in motion any telltale pebbles, and holding his arms crisscrossed in front of his face. Four full strides, and his outstretched hands encountered a bush, and instantly he slid around and crouched behind it.

At just that moment the moon came out from behind its cloud, and once more flooded the mountainside with chalk-like light.

Meanwhile a third voice was saying, "You two goofs give me a pain in the neck, with your imaginings. I wouldn't be at all surprised, when we get back to the cabin, to find that you merely *imagined* Cairns's escape.—There! The moon's out again, and where's your spook?"

"Well, maybe there wasn't anyone there. But I'll bet you a quart, Cairns is gone. You seen him gone, didn't you, Herbert?"

"'Ow c'd Hi 'ave seen 'im if 'e was gone? Hi seen that 'e wasn't there, that's wot you mean."

The voices trailed off, around the corner. Deane came out of his hiding place, and strode on in the opposite direction, chuckling softly.

Said he to himself, "When they get back to their cabin, and find Oscar Cairns sleeping peacefully in his bed, they'll be quite certain that they didn't see me either. So that's okeh."

He reached the spot where he had held the slim tense figure of Mavis Maitland so tenderly in his arms, and he paused there to live that moment over again in memory.

Thus he came down the mountain side into the clearing, on the slopes of which stood the hunting-lodge and its attendant cabins, and the newly built laboratory and storehouse for stratium, and the barracks for the workingmen.

The lodge and cabins were in shadow, with the moon hanging above and beyond the hill on which they stood; but the other buildings were clearly limned in the chalklike light. And down at one end of the flying-field in the valley, the hangar which housed Maitland's planes stood like a black and white toy building-block, flanked by purple shadow.

Deane sighed. He had loved his work here. Thanks to Maitland's millions, he had here done chemical experimentation on a scale never dreamed of by him before!

Not only had he loved the work, but also he had loved the clear crisp air of the North Dakota mountains, and—he smiled wryly to himself at the thought—John Maitland's daughter.

AND NOW HE was about to leave it all. For why? Merely because he had been tricked into coming here. What of it? Tricked into safety. Tricked into work which he enjoyed. Tricked into the intimate companionship of a most exquisite bit of femininity. If this be treason, make the most of it.

Then he thought of Donna Cairns. Poor little Donna. Deprived of her father. Perhaps on the verge of destitution. Believing her beloved father murdered by him, Charles Deane. No! She could not believe it!

And the certainty that Maitland was up to something diabolical. For if not, why the kidnapping of Cairns, and the tricking of himself and Angus Frazer? And anything diabolical that Maitland might be engaged in would be certain to be diablerie on a gigantic scale, for John Cortlandt Maitland never did anything not grandiose.

Yet why leave these pleasant surroundings, to go into danger on what might be a mere wild-goose chase?

At the thought of the danger, Deane smiled and drew in a deep breath. His mind cleared. His thoughts flashed back to the night before the game in the Rose Bowl. Danger? An uphill fight? That was his meat.

With no more regrets, he crossed the clearing and made his way to the cabin occupied by himself and Angus.

His path led past the main lodge, and as he approached it he heard voices. Ordinarily Charles Deane was no eavesdropper. But having set himself to the task of fathoming Maitland's game, all was grist to his mill.

And furthermore, one of the voices was Maitland's; and the other was—the voice that had talked to him over the telephone the morning he had found Cairn's dead body in his laboratory, the voice that had told him to take the taxicab which had brought him to the brownstone front on Riverside Drive, the house of Maitland.

7

"ICHOR"

CHARLES DEANE WAS dumfounded at now hearing the same voice with which he had talked over the phone after finding the dead body in his laboratory two months ago. A voice he identified later that morning as the voice of the bearded hunched-up man who had been haunting his laboratory. The fact that this same voice was now talking with his patron, John Cortlandt Maitland, was the last bit of evidence necessary to convince Deane that Maitland personally was responsible for all of his troubles.

Accordingly, avoiding the shafts of light which rayed out through the open windows of the hunting lodge, and grateful that he was on the further side of the building from the moon, and hence in purple darkness, he crept forward to listen to what the two men were saying. Not only was he able to listen, but also, without getting in the telltale beams of light, he was able to look into the bright interior.

Maitland sat facing the window, his customary quizzical smile on his bronzed features. Pacing up and down in front of him was a man of about Deane's own age, a lithe handsome dark-haired man. Not at all the bearded hunched-up creature whom Deane had expected to see!

Maitland was saying calmly, and apparently without

rancor, "No one but you, Alpheus, would dare to speak to me in that way, for you alone share with me the secret of immortality."

"It is necessary that someone share it, Chief," the younger man replied, "in order to keep faith with the lesser members of the Order. For even the immortal leader of an order of immortals might suffer accidental death; and if the secret thus became lost, the rest of us would perish. And have I not proved worthy of your trust? Have I not served you loyally, in spite of my not agreeing with your policies? I still believe that we could afford to wait."

"Yes," said Maitland levelly, but with just a touch of a sneer in his tone, "wait like a clam, only to meet accidental death as did our former chief. What is the use of living forever, unless one begins actually to *live?* 'Forever' is a long, long time; and I want to live now, in the present. That's why I revised the motto of our Order."

"As for me," Alpheus replied, shaking his head, "I would rather sit quietly, and study and learn, while my money doubles every thirty years, and the world gradually gets to be a better place to live in. Thus, when finally I become a multi-millionaire by the mere accumulation of compound interest, I shall be fully prepared to enjoy myself in a world at last fully developed to entertain me."

Maitland smiled, and his eyes flashed, as he drew a deep breath. "As for me, I crave action," he asserted. "Why wait?"

The tall dark young man suddenly ceased his pacing up and down, and clenched his fists. "I crave Mavis," he almost hissed.

Maitland cocked his head slightly on one side, pursed his lips, narrowed his eyelids, and nodded ruminatively. To

*Deane found the man's
wrist just in time*

the watcher in the purple shadows outside the window, it
was impossible to judge whether the mood of this master
mind was menacing or merely amused.

"So?" purred Maitland. "I thought I told you, Alpheus,
to lay off of Mavis."

"But why, Chief? *She* is one of us. *I* am one of us. That
fool of a yellow-haired young chemist is *not.*"

"*She* is yellow-haired. *Jones* is yellow-haired. You are
not," mocked Maitland. "I take it, Alpheus, that you do not
believe in the Nordic theory."

"But why do you persist in playing with this Deane
person? Might just as well call him by his real name, seeing
as both of us know who he is. Why do you continue to
play with him? He has given you this new metal, stratium;
which is all that you needed of him."

"I'm not so sure," ruminated Maitland. "He is keen. I
like him. Mavis likes him, too—"

The younger man threw out his hands with a gesture of despair.

Maitland continued relentlessly, "And so I've about made up my mind to offer him life everlasting."

"But what of me?" Alpheus exploded.

"My friend," said Maitland levelly, "you surprise me. Can the gods know love? Passion, yes, and passing fancy; but not love. Love is a biological urge, and can have no place alongside of immortality."

Charles Deane's mind was racing, in an attempt to keep pace with this weird conversation. It was all so utterly absurd, this talk of immortality, as though such things were possible. And yet it was so characteristic of Maitland as to be wholly plausible.

The two men in the lighted room had ceased talking, and were merely confronting each other, staring into each other's faces; so that the watcher outside in the shadows of the moonlit night had a few moments in which to sum up his thoughts.

A SECRET SOCIETY of persons who at least believed themselves to be immortals! With that as a clue, the whole jig-saw puzzle of the last few months slipped into place. The strange personality and masterful power of John Cortlandt Maitland. The kidnapings and murders. The altered motto on the wall of the hunting lodge. All fitted into one complete picture of ruthless determination to dominate the world, and of ability to realize that project.

And running through it all, as a connecting pattern, was the strange crimson oxygen-scented "blood." Ichor of the gods, perhaps. Why not?

Deane smiled wryly to himself at the incongruity of

him, a scientist, believing such rot. Then crammed his ear to catch the words which Alpheus, in a lowered voice, was now speaking to Maitland. But another voice, sweet and feminine, came to his senses from the dark shadows beside him.

"Charles, dear," it said.

He wheeled, and was about to make some involuntary exclamation, when cool fingertips were laid upon his lips, and a firm slim hand gripped one of his shoulders.

Silhouetted against the moonlit mountainside, he saw the vibrant form of Mavis Maitland standing close to him; and with a sudden urge, he flung his arms around her, and drew her unresistant to him. This was not for that dark-haired Alpheus, if he could help it.

Long and silently they embraced in the purple shadows, while, less than twenty feet away, all unknowing of their presence, two others plotted and planned against them.

At length she disengaged herself.

Then, inviting him with a slight sideward nod of her trim head, "Come!" said she; and taking his hand, led him along the side of the hunting lodge, and to her own cabin.

"Come in," said she. "I want to talk to you." So together they entered.

She was still clad in the filmy white and moon-green of their walk together of earlier that evening; but now, instead of her usual steel-cold poise and self-assurance, she seemed warmly palpitatingly human. Even the cat-yellow eyes beneath her penciled brows seemed for once to have abandoned their intriguing aloofness, and to have become frankly appealing. Deane gasped. Never had he seen her so beautiful.

He held out his arms to her, and once more she swept forward toward him. But just short of his embrace she paused, and wistfully shook her head.

"Just a moment, dear," said she. "Let's talk a moment first."

And gently eluding him, she sank into a chair, and motioned him to another nearby.

"And let us not repeat the error of my father and Alpheus," she continued, "Let us talk in whispers, for fear of eavesdroppers. Fortunately the windows and door of this sitting room are on the moonlit side, and so there is not much danger of any one drawing near unseen."

"Mavis, Mavis, Mavis. Beautiful Mavis," breathed Deane.

"The cold impersonal scientist," she bantered. Then sobering, "And yet, being a scientist, and having heard what you have heard, you already know too much. It would go hard with you if father were to learn that you had been listening at his window,"

"And you would tell him?"

"I might, if it suited my ends," she replied with a trace of her characteristic steeliness.

"I don't like you that way," said Deane soberly.

"Forgive me, dear," said she, coloring slightly. "And now we had best understand each other. Just how much *do* you know?"

"Well, for example," Deane thoughtfully replied, "I know that your father is the head of a secret order of some sort, that that Alpheus person is a member, that they believe themselves to be immortal, and that the secret of their supposed immortality lies in some chemical substance in

their blood. The 'ichor' of Greek mythology, which flowed
in the veins of the ancient gods."

MAVIS WATCHED HIM intently as he spoke. Then she
remarked, "You know considerably more than you have
either seen or heard. That is the scientist in you. I like to
watch your mind work. Well, knowing as much as you do,
there is no harm in your knowing a little more.—Do you
really love me?"

Seizing her hand, he exclaimed, "Mavis, dear, I do, I do.
Oh, Mavis, could you marry a nobody like me?" She smiled
a cool smile, like a moonlit ripple.

"I have been waiting for those words," said she.

"But could you? Would you?" he persisted.

"Do you think," she retorted, "that I would have surren-
dered utterly to your kisses if I did not love you as you love
me?"

"Then I shall go to your father—" he exulted.

"And tell him that you will join our Order?"

"You mean—?"

"That you and I shall be together always—forever and
ever. Isn't that a beautiful thought? Eternal love! And I
had feared that it was impossible, that love and immortality were incompatible. Father has always taught so.
Yet Alpheus is immortal, and he loves—loves me deeply.
And if he can love, then so can you. Oh, it is going to
be beautiful, exquisite—our love together. Kiss me, kiss
me, Charles." She leaned forward, pulsing with life. Then
recoiled abruptly, as though a glass of ice water had been
dashed in her face.

"Oh, Charles!" she cried. "Don't! Don't look at me that
way! Oh, that look of horror on your face! Horror and

repulsion! A moment ago you said you loved me. And now you hate me, loathe me. Why? Why?"

"Oh!" groaned Deane, burying his face, in his hands. "Mavis, Mavis, forgive me. You aren't real. You aren't human. You're a *thing!* You're a *robot!* I thought you were a woman, and—God help me—I loved you."

"Charles Deane," said she, her face expressionless, her yellow eyes narrowed and catlike, "you can never know how you have hurt me. Your face, even more than your words. Never to my dying day—"

She smiled wryly, and amended it to, "Never, through all eternity, shall I forget that look of utter revulsion in your eyes. When you are old, and gray, and dead—and I am still as you see me now—that look shall still haunt me. If you could do that look to order, you could make a fortune with it on the screen. Well, it should be a lesson to me. Gods ought not to stoop, to mate with mortals."

"But, Mavis, Mavis dear—"

She shook her head. "It is over," said she. "*Our* love is over. But not *my* love for you. What do you want, more than anything else in the world?"

He raised haggard eyes to hers. "I want *you,* Mavis—"

But again she shook her head.

"No," she said decidedly. "*That* is over. What you want is to get away from here. To get out of the toils of the Order, before the Order engulfs you and turns *you* into a 'thing' like us. And so, I'm going to spare you, and help you to escape, although I feel confident that if I kept you here, I could win you in the end."

"Mavis," he breathed, "you're a brick!"

"I was afraid so," she retorted grimly. "Meet me here just before sunrise, and I'll get you out."

Once more he held out his arms to her, but she sadly shook her head.

"Go!" said she. He went.

IT WAS NOW well past midnight. At his own cabin he roused Angus Frazer, and spent the rest of the night in telling the old Scotsman as much as he thought advisable of the present situation.

But he had scarcely embarked on the story when Angus interrupted with, "And how much have you had to drrink. Sirr?"

"I don't blame you in the least," said Deane, "but it's true, and you've got to listen. You know, we've often tried to piece all this mess together, and now at last everything fits. Cairns is alive. I've a letter here from him to his daughter. I'm going to get out of here—Mavis Maitland has agreed to help me. You're going to sit tight, keep your eyes and ears open, and wait for word from either Cairns or me. If any one asks you anything about my whereabouts, you just plain don't know. I was still out when you went to bed. I had returned and gone before you got up. My bed has been slept in—that's all you know. We'd better go and muss it up right now."

They did so.

Then Deane resumed, "Remember how we worked over that blood sample on the handkerchief which 'the face' dropped by the door of our laboratory. Remember my telling you that I got smeared with some of the same stuff in my fight in the taxicab. I got some more of the same on my own handkerchief when I—"

He paused and flushed guiltily, then finished lamely, "Well, it's the clue to the whole business. It's 'ichor.'"

Frazer had dourly raised his eyebrows at Deane's hesitation and flush; but now, diverted, he exclaimed, "It's what?"

"Ichor," Deane repeated. "Ichor of the immortal gods."

"Now I *know* you'rre drrunk," said the Scotsman.

But when Deane concluded his explanation, even old Angus believed.

"Whateverr they'rre up to, it's forr no good," said he. "I'm with you, sirr. But don't be trrusting any women."

Deane smiled. He had not told his assistant his reasons for believing that he could rely on Mavis Maitland implicitly.

Final arrangements were made.

"Watch for blood samples," he commanded. "Check all the oxides and all the red pigments in the laboratory here, and perhaps you'll get a clue as to how they make this ichor."

Then he shaved and changed his clothing.

The sky was just beginning to turn gray over the mountain tops, when he extinguished the lights, opened the door of the cabin, and peered cautiously out. The moon had set, but in the early morning light he was dimly able to make out the dark form of a man seated on a huge bowlder not twenty feet away!

However, the man gave no indication of having seen or heard the opening of the door. Quietly Deane closed it again, and whispered to Angus, "Man outside."

Together the two friends tiptoed into the back bedroom. All was darkness and silence. The window was open, screened with cloth netting. Whipping out his knife,

Deane cleared this obstruction away. Then, after shaking Frazer's hand in mute good-by, he quietly lowered himself over the sill, and began groping his way along the mountainside.

"I'm sorry, Mr. Jones," spoke a gruff voice out of the darkness. "Mr. Maitland's orders are that no one is to leave your cabin."

8

WAR IN THE AIR

TAKEN COMPLETELY BY surprise though he was, Deane lunged forward and drove his clenched fist full at the spot from which the sound of the voice had come. The man was nearer than Deane had thought. There was a muffled oath, and then a dull thud as the man staggered backward and fell. Then no further sound.

"Must have struck his head on a rock," said Deane to himself, as he groped hurriedly forward through the darkness.

"Halt!" peremptorily shouted the familiar voice of Alpheus ahead of him. "Halt, or I fire! I have an automatic."

Deane stopped abruptly. "I don't think Mr. Maitland would care for that," he coolly replied. "Besides, I can't see you in this darkness, and so I doubt if you can see me."

"Oh, yes I can," retorted the voice, "for you are silhouetted against the sky."

Deane instantly dropped to the ground. "You can't now," said he, seizing a stone in one hand, and then springing catlike to one side.

There came a flash and a roar from the automatic, and almost simultaneously Deane heaved his rock in the direction of the flash.

But it clattered on the mountainside, and the mocking voice answered, "No go. I can step aside, as well as you. And now I'll give you one more chance, although personally I'd much rather kill you. Stand up and hold your hands above your head. Otherwise I'll just sit here until I hear the scratch of gravel, and then I'll fire at the sound. I'm a pretty accurate shot, Charles Deane."

Deane made no reply, but cautiously groped about him for another stone. Banding one, he tossed it to one side. Instantly the automatic spoke again.

"Two shots," said Deane to himself. "He has only five more, and then he'll have to reload."

But the voice spoke again from the darkness, "I saw you that time by the light of the flash of my gun. A cute trick, tossing that pebble. But it won't work again. Next time I shall fire twice: once at your pebble, and once at you. Better surrender, before I get fed up with you."

Meanwhile Deane was groping for another rock. He found two. Tossing one with his left hand, he poised expectant; and, when the flash came, heaved the other. He heard it thud, as it struck his enemy. Then came a second flash and roar, and a bullet brushed his sleeve.

Deane flung himself one side, as the third flash came.

"Five shots," said Deane to himself. "He has only two more."

Silence.

The sound of a click, and then the voice of Alpheus, "In case you are depending on my using up my seven shots, and then your rushing me, it may interest you to know that I've just inserted another magazine. Better surrender."

"All right," said Deane, "here goes."

And with that he sprang at the sound of the voice. He found the man's right wrist just in time. Twice more the pistol spoke, and then Deane bent the wrist backward, until the hand released its grip,

Mystery Man

and the pistol clattered to the rocks. Deane drove forward with his fist at where he imagined his opponent's solar-plexus to be, and met soft flesh. The body slipped away from him, and thudded to the ground.

Stooping swiftly, Deane swept his hand over the surface of the rocks, and recovered the automatic.

From the darkness at his feet there came the unmistakable straining groan of a winded man, trying to regain his breath.

Pointing the gun at the sound, Deane announced, "So much for you, Alpheus. I have you covered. As soon as you catch your breath, tell me that you surrender.

"I'll give you a reasonable length of time, and then I'll fire. I'd hate to have to kill an immortal."

The groaning continued. Then it stopped abruptly.

"No monkey business!" Deane warned.

Then the calm voice of Alpheus spoke, "Your gun isn't

loaded. I lied to you about the second clip. Feel of the gun with your left hand, and you'll see that the slide is back."

Deane did so. It was.

Alpheus continued, "But I do have a second gun. You are silhouetted against the sky. I have you covered. In your own words, 'no monkey business.' Put up your hands." Deane did so.

"Now march to your cabin. You see, Deane, where your scientific mind failed you was in not remembering that we immortals do not have to breathe. So it does no good to hit one of us in the solar-plexus. You should have tried the chin."

Deane walked with apparent meekness, but alert for a break, around the cabin to the front door.

"Hey, Jenks," called Alpheus.

"If you mean the man who was guarding the rear window," Deane informed him, "he's out cold."

"Oh, very well," said his captor. "Hey, there, Frazer inside. Turn on the lights. I'm armed, and—"

His voice ended in a sudden gurgle. Deane wheeled.

"I've got him, Sirr," spoke Angus Frazer out of the darkness. "Quick, snatch his gun while I hold him."

BUT ALPHEUS WAS unarmed. His second gun had been pure bluff. In the strong arms of the two scientists, he was helpless; and soon they had him inside the cottage, firmly bound and gagged. They lit up. Then with a flashlight they found the body of the other guard, and brought it in and trussed it up too. It was limp and unbreathing.

"Don't worry about that," said Deane. "These immortals never breathe unless they happen to think of it. His heart is still beating."

Alpheus glared at them malevolently, and mumbled something beneath his gag.

"Well, Sirr," said Angus, "Who have we the honorr of enterrtaining?"

"This one is Alpheus," said Deane, grinning, "the second in command on Mt. Olympus. I don't know the other, but his name appears to be 'Jenks.'"

Frazer sighed. "I guess I'll have to go with you, Sirr," said he. "Forr, if I correctly rrememberr my mythology, it's not altogetherr healthy to truss up one of the immorrtals."

A sudden glance by Alpheus past them, caused both men to wheel suddenly and face the door.

There, in a trim form-fitting white corduroy aviation costume, stood Mavis Maitland.

"Well," said she scornfully, "you seem to have messed things up pretty thoroughly."

"Me?" exclaimed Deane in a surprised aggrieved tone.

"No," said she sweetly. "My friend Alpheus here."

The prisoner mumbled something, and his dark eyes snapped fire.

"I don't get your words, but I catch the general drift," said Mavis. "You are wrong, my friend. Father will do nothing of the sort. And the next time that you wish to interfere with my plans, may I suggest that you first speak to father, instead of trying to handle the matter yourself in your usual clumsy fashion." Then to Deane and Frazer, "Come on. We've got to hurry. But let's first make sure that our two captives are securely tied."

So saying, she stepped into the room, and deftly inspected the knots. This brisk efficient Mavis was quite different from her usual cat-sleepy daytime self. "They'll do," said she.

Then, snapping off the lights, she led the way out of the cabin. The first streaks of dawn were showing over the mountain tops, and by now it was light enough to pick one's way across the rocks. Running lightly, Mavis Maitland made for the level floor of the valley, followed by Deane and Frazer.

The doors of the airplane hangar were open, and a small white Wasp plane stood in readiness with mechanics bustling around it.

Waving her hand toward the rear seat, she said in a low tone, "Get in quickly." Then, in a louder tone to one of the mechanics, as she clambered in herself, "I start at once."

"All ready, miss," said he.

She fingered the controls and called out, "Contact!"

One of the attendants spun the propeller. She sped it up to a roar, and the ship pushed against its skids, and tilted forward. She slowed the motor down again, and looked around. Deane and Frazer were wedged tightly into the rear seat.

Somewhere in the distant dark recesses of the hangar a telephone rang. A voice answered it. Mavis slowed her motor almost to a stall, cocked her pretty head on one side, and listened.

Then, in a sudden panic, she shouted, above the din of the motor, "Clear!"

"But, miss," called back one of the mechanics, "hadn't you better—"

"Clear, I said!" she shouted peremptorily.

The skids were pulled aside, the motor sped up, and the ship taxied slowly out of the door.

Men came running from the rear of the hangar.

"Stop!" one of them shouted." It's the boss's orders."

A blast from the propeller swept him off his feet, but one of his companions seized the tail of the craft and hung on for all he was worth. Thus weighted, it would be impossible for the ship to rise.

BEFORE EITHER DEANE or Miss Maitland realized what he was about, Angus Frazer had leaped over the side. Falling to the ground as he landed, he struggled to his feet, and grabbed at the legs of the mechanic as he swept by.

The mechanic loosened his hold with one hand to strike at his assailants, and lost the grip of the other. Together the two men rolled in the dust.

Suddenly freed of the weight on its tail, the ship took a forward dip, but Mavis pulled back the joy-stick, righted the ship, and then took off the ground.

As she circled, to gain altitude in the narrow valley, she passed close over the hangar. Another ship had been wheeled out, and Angus Frazer was fighting his way toward it through a group of mechanics. He was still on his feet and still fighting, as Mavis and Deane passed out of sight over the rim of the valley.

Mavis turned her head back, and smiled at her passenger.

"Good old Angus," Deane shouted. "Never thinks of himself."

"It's just as well," Mavis shouted back. "Father is going to give us a run for it, and we can spare that extra weight."

She turned her head back, banked sharply, and set her course to the westward.

"They'll expect me to fly east," she called back in explanation. "The nearest landing field is in *that* direction."

And sure enough, when the black ship of their pursuers
finally rose from the valley, it was headed east.

But it quickly learned its mistake, and circled to follow
them.

"Step on it!" shouted Deane.

The girl gave her ship everything that she had, but gradually the pursuing craft gained on them, until it hung just
above and behind their tail. And there it stayed. Deane
looked up and hack, and saw a machine-gun menacingly
pointed at him over the side of the ship above.

"Duck and crawl forward!" shouted Mavis.

And, just as he did so, the machine-gun let loose a blast.
The little white plane gave a lurch.

"Oh, my dear!" cried Mavis. "Did they hit you?"

With his head close to the girl's feet, Deane looked up
at her.

"I'm all right. Are you?"

"O.K.," she replied. "And so are you as long as you stay
close to me. They'd never risk hitting my father's daughter."

"I figured as much," grinned Deane, "or I'd never have
taken cover and left you to stand the gaff."

"We're safe so long as we are over the mountains," she
explained. "But as soon as we reach level country, watch
out. They'll try and force us to a landing."

For twenty minutes or so they sped on in silence, save
for the roar of the motors. By now it was broad daylight.

"Well," said Mavis, "here's the end of the hills. First
they'll try to cut off my ignition."

"Shoot it off?" asked Deane.

"No. Counteract it magnetically."

"That's a new one on me," Deane admitted.

"Oh," she airily asserted, "we immortals have made many scientific advances ahead of the rest of the world."

"But now—?"

"I really don't know myself. But, anyway, it won't work on me. At least I hope it won't. For father, fearing that enemies might learn the secret of his motor-stopping ray, has just experimentally installed a hot-bulb ignition on this little boat of mine. There they go."

Her motor began to cough and sputter.

"And here *I* go."

She threw a lever on the instrument board, and her motor picked up again.

A few minutes later she announced, "Well, they've given *that* up. And now they've started to crowd me. A bit more dangerous than the magnetic method, but just as effective. Hold tight! I'm going to loop."

THE FLOOR OF the cockpit suddenly reared up in front of Deane, the ship quivered as though struck; and then it spiraled, bumping Deane against the sides.

"We made it!" the girl shouted. "A half backward loop and a side slip. They grazed our tail, and they nearly lost control. Had to dive to avoid hitting us. They're nearly down to the ground by now, and we're going up and up. Crawl back into your seat and take a look."

Deane did so. Mavis was driving the Wasp upward at a sharp angle, and far below them, headed at right angles to their course, was the black ship of their pursuers, still falling.

The country was level farming land, and far off ahead lay the fluttering pennons of an airport.

"You're a brick!" shouted Deane, but Mavis merely glanced back, pouted up her lips and sniffed. Then Deane remembered that the last time he had uttered that sentiment it hadn't set so well.

He glanced overside again. The driver of the enemy ship appeared by now to have recovered his shattered nerves. He had turned in their direction, and was rising again.

Mavis meanwhile had taken out a little telescope with a vertical circular gauge on it, and was sighting ahead at the airport. Then nodding her head in a satisfied manner, she replaced the instrument in a flap-pocket, shut off her motor, and headed down.

There is no more sickening sound than that of a diving plane. Deane winced and held onto the sides of the cockpit.

Mavis glanced back, smiled, caught his agonized expression and gaily laughed aloud.

"You watch the enemy for me," she commanded. "I've got to keep both eyes on the airport."

Deane turned his attention to the black ship below and behind him, and soon forgot the sensation and the sound of falling.

Finally he announced, "They're gaining. They're a bit ahead of us."

Mavis took one look, then glanced back at her passenger. Her eyes were slits. Her little chin was firm.

"Power dive," she shouted, and cut in the motor again.

With a roar, the ship shot forward. The stays shrieked ominously. Deane glanced up just in time to see a piece of covering rip off the wing. But the girl merely gave the ship more gun and kept on.

9

CRASH!

DEANE LOOKED OVERSIDE; the black craft of their pursuers was being left behind. He looked ahead; the rapidly widening airport was rushing up at them.

"O.K.," he shouted. "We've lost them!"

Mavis shut off the motor, nosed up, circled, and brought the ship down into the wind in a perfect landing. The black ship veered off, and disappeared behind a clump of trees.

Deane sprang out, and assisted his companion to alight.

"Well," she gayly announced, "we made it."

Then swayed against him, and collapsed in his arms. But in a few moments she opened her eyes, and smiled dewily up at him.

"Forgive me, Charles, dear," said she. "I can't faint now."

"It's all right, dear. Go right ahead, if you want to," he encouraged.

"I mean it literally," she said, standing erect. "We, who live forever, cannot faint."

He looked at her sternly, and sadly shook his head.

"Why did you remind me that you are—?" he began.

"Perhaps on purpose."

"All aboard for the mail-plane east!" blared out the loud speakers.

"Just a minute," she called out to the pilot. "We must buy our tickets."

"It's all right with me, lady," said he, surveying her appreciatively. "After that landing that you made, I'll be proud to have you fly with me."

"You are going, too, Mavis?" breathed Deane hopefully, as they hurried together over to the ticket office. Then his face fell, as he added with sudden afterthought, "But I have no money. No money at all."

"I have plenty of money. Plenty for us both," she replied.

He brightened, but she continued, "But I cannot go with you, I cannot subject you to a life of horror, wedded to a 'thing.' No, no," as he started to protest. "What's done is done, and what's said is said. One ticket through to New York." This to the man at the window. "And here are two hundred dollars for emergencies, and here is a gun." She handed over a little pearl-handled 30-caliber Lüger automatic.

At the steps of the mail-plane, she held out her hand to Deane.

"Goodby and good luck," said she.

"What! Ain't yer goin' with us, lady?" complained the pilot.

"Not this time," she sweetly replied.

"Please come!" Deane begged. For a moment she hesitated.

"Come on, lady," urged the pilot.

But she resolutely shook her head.

She was standing below, waving to them, as the plane took off.

Deane was the only passenger. The plane was a relatively

small one, with no attendants. Deane sat by the window and stared moodily out, until the airport, with its tiny white waving figure, disappeared in the distance behind them. Then he glanced up, and swept the sky with his gaze. Just as he expected: the black scout plane was following them.

So he walked forward and spoke to the pilot, "I just thought I ought to tell you that there's an air bandit following us."

The pilot looked up at him and grinned.

"Quit your kidding," said he.

"Don't say I didn't warn you," said Deane, returning to his seat.

The black plane continued to gain until it came alongside. Its pilot waved to the mail pilot until he attracted his attention, and then pointed downward with a forcible gesture. The mail pilot shook his head. Whereupon the black plane once more unlimbered its machine gun. Deane promptly dropped to the floor, and crawled forward.

"What did I tell you?" said he.

"You'd better get ready to bail out," was the reply. "Parachutes are under the rear seat. Directions on the package. If they get me, open the door and fall out backward. When clear of the ship, count three *very* slowly, and then pull the rip-cord."

"But, man, it's me they're after, not you," Deane guiltily objected.

"That's all right. It's all in the day's work. You do as you're told. And anyway, they're probably bluffing. No one would dare to shoot down the U.S. mail in broad daylight."

Deane crept back, found the parachutes and adjusted one on his shoulders. Then he looked forward at the pilot, who just at that moment was thumbing his nose out the window. There followed a couple of bursts of machine gun fire, barely discernible above the roar of the motors; and a sputter of glass above Deane's head.

The pilot shouted back reassuringly, "They're just trying to scare me, but it doesn't work."

And then the motor stopped.

The pilot worked violently with his instrument board.

No use," Deane shouted. "They've cut off your ignition with a magnetic ray."

"Hell!" ejaculated the pilot. "Then you'd better jump. Though I'll *try* to make a landing."

The soul-chilling wheeee of a motorless falling plane smote on Deane's ears as he staggered erect and groped for the door.

The last thing that he remembered was frantically trying to turn the handle. But the door would not open.

THE NEXT THING he knew, he was lying in a most uncomfortable position, bruised and scratched. Nearby could be heard the crackling of flames. He opened his eyes, and something sharp struck into one of them, causing it to water profusely, and nearly blinding him. He tried to turn over in bed, and was poked with sharp sticks in a dozen places.

He was about to groan with pain, when some sixth sense restrained him. His arms seemed tied to his sides, but finally he found that by patient effort he could move them through the obstructions which held them, until at last he got both hands shifted to a protective position in front of his eyes. Then cautiously he opened his eyes again.

He was lying in a thick brush, through the branches of

which he could just barely make out the rough outlines of the scene before him; the mail plane, nose down and tail in air, blazing hotly away; and a safe distance to one side of it, the black plane of the immortals.

Two figures in aviation helmets scouted around between his bush and the blazing pyre, and he heard one of them say, "I could swear I saw some one fall clear. But I guess I'm wrong. There are no survivors."

"It's just as well," rejoined the other. "Dead men tell no tales."

Then they passed on, around the fire, and back to their own plane. The motor started again, and they were off.

Deane waited, in an agony both physical and mental, until the black plane became a mere dot in the sky, before he stirred. Then very cautiously he stood up, and took an inventory of himself. Scratched and bruised and lame though he was, nothing appeared to be broken. So, slipping the still unopened parachute-pack from his shoulders, he tossed it into the dying blaze of the mail plane.

"Sunk without trace, eh?" said he grimly. "Well, so be it. Let the pursuit end right here. Later I may decide to be a witness for Uncle Sam, but not just now." Then, as a sudden thought assailed him, "And thank God that Mavis did not come along! I hope she doesn't blame herself for my death. I'll get word to her, as soon as I'm safe in New York."

So saying, he started limping across the prairie toward a line of telephone poles which he saw in the distance.

The poles proved to indicate a railroad, and along this he trudged eastward. The sun rose in the sky. The day got hot and hotter. Deane lost all track of time, as he stumbled on.

He was practically out on his feet, when a noise behind

him gradually began to obtrude itself upon his senses. Suddenly awake and alert once more, he recognized the noise as the puffing of a freight train, a freight train slowly climbing an upgrade. He looked around—he had left the prairie behind him.

The sound of the train came from the westward, so Deane hurried ahead, until he reached some bushes by a culvert, and there he lay and hid.

He had difficulty in keeping awake, and in fact was just dozing off, when the arrival of the freight awakened him. It was a long freight, and was moving very slowly. So, as soon as the engine was safely by, Deane crawled from his place of concealment, ran alongside, and swung aboard.

NEVER HAD HE ridden a freight before, but he had read about such things in the magazines, and so he knew that underneath the cars there were parts called "brake-beams," upon which beams hoboes comfortably ensconce themselves for transcontinental trips. So he stepped around onto the ladder which ran up the end of one of the cars between it and the next car. Then scrunched down, and peered beneath the car.

But there was nothing there to resemble even remotely his idea of "brake-beams." The nearest object in view was the rotating axle which connected the two rear wheels of the car. Beyond that was the solid structure of the rear truck, completely obstructing any forward passage beneath the car, and in itself affording no place whatever on which to sit or lie.

It occurred to him as a bit embarrassing that he, a scientist and hence supposedly a keen observer, had never taken note before of the exact construction of a freight ear.

*Stepping forward, he
lunged at the polieman*

Running one hand several times through his tousled sandy
hair, he cogitated for a moment; then shifted his footing
to the stirrup on the outside of the car, and peered ahead
of the rear truck. Nothing there either on which to sit or
lie. So he swung back between the cars.

As he remembered the train, as viewed from his recent
hiding place in the bushes, it contained no flat cars, no
tank cars, and no coal cars. No cars of any sort on which he
could find a comfortable resting place. And even if there

had been such a car, he would certainly be discovered on it by the brakemen of the train.

Then he remembered that one of the side doors on the car ahead of the one on which he was now riding had been slightly ajar. So he clambered to the top of the ladder, and poking his head cautiously above the level of the car-tops, he glanced hurriedly in both directions. None of the train crew in sight.

So he finished the ascent, and ran along the top of his car and the next one ahead. Then lay down and crawled to the edge. Yes, the side door was a few inches open. Reaching over, he pushed it open about two feet; then, backing over the edge, he swung himself through the opening and landed on the floor of the car.

It was empty, save for some excelsior, hay, and pieces of burlap; so, first closing the door again, he gathered a pile of this material together, and lay down on it for a much needed sleep.

The next thing that he knew, he was awakened by the sliding open of the door of his car. It was dark outside, but the feeble beams of a lantern penetrated the interior. Instantly alert, Deane drew some of the nearby burlap over him, and then lay motionless.

A voice spoke outside, "This one is an empty. You must have got your numbers twisted, Mike."

Then the light disappeared, and departing footsteps on cinders could be heard, growing gradually fainter.

TOSSING OFF THE burlap, Deane crawled to the door of the car and peered out. There were two men, one carrying a lantern and the other a pad of paper, several cars away.

As Deane watched, they swung open the door of the

car they were inspecting, and one after the other crawled into it. Deane immediately jumped down from his car, and tiptoed off into the darkness in the opposite direction.

It was a starlit night, and the moon had not yet risen. All around him loomed the dark shapes of freight cars.

But at length he came to a clear stretch of track and then to a railroad station, on which the name read "Fargo."

His first thought was food, so he made his way to a nearby restaurant, where he perched himself upon a stool and ordered himself a full meal.

WHILE WAITING TO be served, he picked up an evening paper, and glanced idly through it. A headline caught his attention: "Mail Plane Crashes." He read the article; it related the very wreck from which he himself had escaped that morning. It seems that earlier editions had reported merely that the plane had failed to reach its next stop. Later, a westbound plane had sighted the smoking wreckage, and had come down to investigate. The remains of only one body had been found. Yet the plane had carried two persons, namely the aviator, and one male passenger (name unknown), who had purchased a through ticket for New York.

Considerable speculation was rife as to which of the two had escaped death, and as to what had become of the survivor. Footprints had been found, constituting a winding trail from near the scene of the crash to a nearby railroad track, but there the trail had vanished. It was assumed that the survivor, badly burned and partly crazed by his burns, had wandered that far, and then down the tracks in one direction or the other, and had probably been struck by a train, or fallen off a trestle or down an embankment. Squads of volunteers were now making a thorough search.

"And I'll bet that representatives of the Maitland gang are in each of those squads," Deane added to himself, with a grim smile.

At this juncture the white-coated man behind the counter shoved his soup in front of him, so he laid down the paper, and picked up his spoon. As he began to eat, he glanced up and down the counter.

The next customer to his right, several seats away, was a swarthy heavy-set Sicilian with a huge black mustache. This man was eying him intently, even malevolently, it seemed, as he looked up. Deane hurriedly turned his eyes back to his soup, but the Sicilian kept up his intent stare.

A momentary panic seized Deane. Was this swarthy man a henchman of Maitland? But instantly Deane realized that if this were so, then all the more important for him to be calm; so he devoted himself, as nonchalantly as possible, to his meal; and did not even cast a glance in the direction of his neighbor.

But, though he ate with simulated calm, he was rapidly developing a plan of action.

Sooner or later—perhaps it had happened already—something would be found on or about the charred body in the wrecked plane to identify it as that of the pilot; and then Maitland would know that Deane had escaped. Not finding Deane's body beside the right-of-way, Maitland would cause his far-flung organization to guard and search all sizeable towns in both directions along the railroad—undoubtedly the master-mind had already foreseen not finding Deane on the right-of-way, and was already taking this precaution. Why, undoubtedly the Sicilian was a part of this program!

Involuntarily Deane glanced to the right, but his neighbor was now engrossed in a bowl of spaghetti.

Deane continued his planning, meanwhile devoting himself to his own food. From the published item about Deane's through air-line ticket to New York, Maitland would know his destination, Maitland's henchmen would be set to watch all forms of transportation leading into the metropolis. Accordingly, Deane's problem would be to elude these watchers, and reach the house of Donna Cairns ahead of them.

He thrust his hand into his pocket, and was reassured by the touch of the little pearl-handled Lüger of Mavis Maitland. A face swam before his eyes, a confusing face, framed in honey-colored hair; or was it brown? Cat-yellow—no, frank blue—eyes. Steel-cold—or wistful—smile. Was it the face of Mavis Maitland, or of Donna Cairns? Deane shook his head, and passed the fingers of one hand through his tousled sandy hair.

THEN HE RESUMED his planning. His first job was to find out about train, plane and bus schedules. His second job was to throw the Sicilian off the track.

Finishing and paying for his meal, he left the restaurant. The Sicilian followed him. Some of the stores were still open. Abruptly Deane decided to kill two birds with one stone; so he entered one of the stores, and bought a small grip, pajamas, shirts, socks, and a toilet kit. The Sicilian did not enter with him, and was nowhere in sight when he emerged.

Hurriedly taking a taxi, to throw off further pursuit, he directed the driver, "Take me to a good hotel."

The driver took him to the Gardner. There he consulted the railroad guide and the airplane schedules. Only one plane east a day, at 5:10. No go; about twenty hours to wait. The next train for Chicago left at ten minutes before midnight, arriving at 7:10 the next evening. He had had no idea that Fargo was nearly as far as New York from Chicago.

Well, he had better take the train. Next, to throw off the scent any one who might be listening. So, after pretending to shake his head sadly over the train and air schedules, he asked for a bus table, consulted it, smiled broadly, and inquired how far away was the bus terminal.

Then remembering that he had nothing but large bills left of the money which Mavis had given him, he got some change at the desk. Then ostentatiously hailed a taxi for the Greyhound depot.

But, as soon as the yellow was under way, he leaned forward, and in a low tone changed his destination to the Northern Pacific. The driver glanced at him peculiarly, and then cut through an alley.

"Fine!" thought Deane, settling back in his seat, and starting to plan what to do to render himself inconspicuous between now and train time.

The next thing that he knew, the taxi had come to a stop. Deane stared out. All was in darkness. The headlights of the car were off. The driver had alighted, and was opening the door.

"Here you are, sir," he said obsequiously.

"Is this the N.P.?" Deane asked incredulously.

"Yes, sir," said the taxi man.

In a flash, Deane sensed that it was not; but with a perfect attempt at clumsy bewilderment, he shook his head, and then backed out of the cab.

The muzzle of an automatic was jabbed into his ribs, and the voice of the taxi driver hissed in his ear, "Stick 'em up, and hand over your bill-fold."

10

STRUGGLING EASTWARD

HAVING A PISTOL jabbed in one's ribs as one dismounts from a taxi in a dark alley may not seem to be an adequate cause for rejoicing, and yet Deane's heart gave a leap of pleasure as he heard the taxi driver hiss: "Stick 'em up! Hand over your bill-fold."

For instantly he realized that this was just an ordinary holdup, and not a machination of Maitland. And he had expected the jab of the firearm in his ribs; that is just why he had backed out of the cab.

"Yes, yes," he faltered. "Don't shoot."

And at the same instant, with that speed and elusiveness which had made him the Nemesis of Southern California in the Rose Bowl, he pivoted on his right heel and drove his left fist into where he imagined the face of the taxi driver would be.

The fist grazed the other man's cheek. The pistol went off. But, wrenched aside by Deane's sudden twirl, its bullet did not even graze him. Then, guided by where his left fist had touched the man's face, his right fist squarely met the point of the man's jaw. A dull thud was heard, as the man fell inertly backward in the darkness. Promptly Deane stepped over to the cab to retrieve his traveling bag. He could not afford to stick around for police questioning.

But as he reached into the interior two dark forms jumped him from behind. It was well for him that there were two of them, for they collided and interfered with each other. A descending blackjack, intended for his head, missed its mark and landed on his right shoulder.

Deane kicked savagely behind him, heard a grunt of pain, and then wheeled to face his two new assailants. His left hand he raised defensively across his face, but his right arm hung limp, temporarily paralyzed.

One of the men continued to groan; and, from the direction from which the groans came, appeared to be sitting or lying on the ground. But the other shouted a peremptory command, "Stick 'em up, big boy! I've got you covered."

It was too dark to tell what kind of a weapon the man carried, or even to see him at all. For a moment Deane considered lunging forward, relying on the supposition that, if he could not see the man, then by the same token the man could not see him. But suddenly he reflected that he himself was probably silhouetted against the dim light of the cab.

"O.K.," he replied.

Up went his left hand, but his right still hung limp from the blow of the blackjack.

"Both of them," menacingly.

"But I can't," Deane explained. "Your blackjack got my right arm. It's broken, I think."

"Both of them!" repeated the voice out of the darkness, with even more menace in its tone.

A tingle of feeling began to return to the fingers of

Deane's right hand. With a stupendous effort he slowly raised his arm.

The darkness was suddenly penetrated by the ray of a pocket flash light which swept back and forth. It fell on Charles Deane, standing with both hands upraised. It fell upon an inert form in the clothes of a taxi driver, lying flat on his back. It fell on another form, groaning and struggling to rise, with hands braced against the pavement. It fell for just an instant on the man who stood confronting Deane.

And in that instant Deane saw that the man was unarmed; his threat had been mere bluff. The next moment Deane's hands were down and he had lunged forward with his left fist square into the solar-plexus of the man who had tricked him.

Then he wheeled, uncertain how to combat the new menace represented by the flash light.

Again the beam swept over the scene in the alley, and a jovial though authoritative voice said, "Good work, young feller. It's O.K. I'm one of the Fargo police."

And, to prove it, the newcomer turned his flash momentarily on his own blue uniform and shield.

Then the cop continued, "What happened? A holdup?"

"Obviously," Deane replied grimly and a bit nervously.

For the police represented a worse menace to him than any one else short of Maitland's gangsters.

"Turn on the headlights," the policeman commanded.

Deane groped on the dashboard of the cab, and did so; and at once the whole alley became dimly illumined by reflected light. The taxi driver was still out cold, but his two pals were rapidly coming to their senses again. The cop deftly searched them, and then chained them together with a pair of handcuffs. At his direction Deane lifted the driver into the vacant space by the front seat, usually used for baggage. Then the cop and the two prisoners got into the rear, and Deane drove them to the police station.

On the way his mind was working rapidly; so that, when the prisoners were booked, he gave a wholly fictitious name as complaining witness, and stated that he had just arrived in town (luckily they did not ask him on what train), that he had been on his way to the Gardner Hotel when the holdup had occurred, that he had planned to stay in Fargo for several days, and that he would be in court promptly at nine thirty the next morning.

Then he took his bag out of the taxi, walked back to the hotel, and registered by the same false name which he had given at the police station.

ON BEING SHOWN to his room, Deane took the precaution of mussing up his bed and his newly bought pajamas, so that both would look as though they had been slept in. Then he had a refreshing bath and shave and distributed his toilet things about the room.

By this time it was after eleven o'clock. Leaving his room, Deane went out for a walk, located the Northern Pacific Railroad station, and studied its surroundings. Then, returning to the hotel, he asked for his key, announced that he was going to turn in, and left a call for 8 A.M.

Just then the desk clerk was called into the manager's office. Fine! The clerk, if interrogated on the morrow, would swear Deane had gone to bed. There was no one else in the lobby. So Deane slipped out into the street and made for the railroad station.

There he did not buy a ticket, but instead furtively skirted the place and hid in the shadows across the tracks. He chuckled to himself at the thought that, back in his hotel room, his bag contained absolutely nothing which would serve to identify him.

Shortly after half past eleven the eastbound train arrived. Deane sneaked up to it on the side away from the station, and walked the whole length of the train, looking for an opportunity to get on; but there was none. Every door on that side was locked, and he did not dare skirt the rear end.

At length the all-aboards were shouted. There was but one thing to do: Deane crawled onto the steps of one of the Pullman cars and wedged himself there in the tiny space beneath the trapdoor. The train started. He tried to lift the door above his head; but it would not budge.

Smoke and cinders swirled in upon him, nearly choking him. It was with difficulty that he managed to hold on. He knew that he could not stand this very long.

Then he heard a thumping above his head, and voices. Two men were standing in the vestibule of the car, talking. They fumbled with the side door. Their voices sounded louder, as it came open. He saw the streak of light of a cigarette butt flipped out into the night.

The voices departed; the main door of the car slammed. Deane reached up over the edge of the trap, and found that the side door was swinging ajar. So he wormed his way out and over, and soon was standing in the vestibule.

Quietly he closed the side door and then furtively entered the car.

Fortunately the men's washroom was at that end. Deane was a filthy mess. But there was no one in the washroom, and before the porter showed up Deane had shaken out his coat, thoroughly cleaned his face, hair and hands, and turned his shirt inside out, so that he was fairly presentable.

Then he hunted up the Pullman conductor, explained that he had gotten on at the last moment, and booked passage for Chicago.

When Deane was finally in bed in his berth, he could not sleep. Strangely enough, however, instead of worrying about his own predicament, or even turning over in his mind the strenuous affairs of the day, his thoughts reverted to a trim little golden-haired figure in a white aviation costume. There came to his mind a poem which he had once read in a Chicago newspaper:*

> *Star-dust caught in her blown hair one night—*
> *Shaken across the desert from the starry skies—*
> *And the emerald-amethyst world beneath her flight*
> *Shines and dies out in her mysterious eyes.*
> *Feel of the air is in her steel-slim fingers,*
> *And her cool voice is as silver as atmosphere,*
> *While ever and all about her definitely*
> *A sense of space—illimitable—crystal clear.*
> *The path of the planets where four winds meet and pass,*
> *The gold of a comet's trail across the sea,*
> *The shine of the summer sun like gauze of brass,*
> *Are none so intangibly lovely, I think, as she.*

How aptly it described Mavis Maitland! Had she

---

* By courtesy of the Chicago *Tribune*.

returned safely to Sioux Lodge? Had she survived her father's displeasure? Deane wondered.

THE NEXT MORNING at breakfast in the diner he reflected with a grin that the hotel clerk was only just then learning of his absence. But perhaps not even then; for the clerk, upon failing to waken him by phone at eight o'clock, had undoubtedly got into the room by pass-key, and had found that the room had (apparently) been slept in, but that Deane, had arisen early and left the hotel, with the (apparent) intention of returning, as all his belongings were still there. So the clerk wouldn't worry.

No one would worry until court time at nine thirty. If there were other cases ahead of that of his assailants, he would not be missed until that case were reached. Then inquiry would be made at the hotel.

The day would be well along before it would sink in on the Fargo police that he had skipped town. Then the departures on all the morning trains would be checked. It might be several days before it would dawn on the police that he had left the night before.

And if Maitland's gang really were shadowing him in Fargo, they probably would be at least one jump *behind* the Fargo police. Especially if the morning paper had carried an account of the holdup.

So Deane ate his breakfast with considerable relish, feeling quite satisfied with himself. The affair of the taxi-cab, which had seemed for a while to jeopardize his entire get-away, now appeared nothing short of providential.

Nevertheless he took no chances, kept to himself as much as possible, stayed in the smoking room whenever it was unoccupied, ate after the others, and took no promenades on the station platforms.

Nothing eventful occurred throughout the day, but when he returned from the diner after lunch, he found a young man of about his own age sitting in his section, number 2 of car 33. Ordinarily he would have been sufficiently assertive to inform the intruder of the mistake, especially as the intruder was reading Deane's own morning paper— which, by the way, had contained no further news of the plane crash.

But making himself conspicuous was the last thing that Deane desired just then. So, having no belongings in number 2, Deane effacingly withdrew to the smoking room.

As the train was pulling into Chicago, and Deane was standing by the water cooler in the corridor, he happened to overhear just around the partition a snatch of conversation which caused him to prick up his ears.

"Yes," a man's voice was saying, "I occupied number 2 last night. Why?"

"Did you get on at Fargo?" A gruff voice.

"Say, who are you, and just what business is it of yours?"

"I happen to be an inspector of the Chicago police."

A pause, during which Deane pictured to himself the showing of a badge or other credentials. Then an "Oh!" from the first speaker.

The gruff voice repeated its question about getting on at Fargo.

"Certainly not," with some asperity. "I came through from Winnipeg."

"Porter," asked the gruff voice, "did this car come from Winnipeg?"

"No, sah. It hooked on at Fargo, sah."

"And this young man occupied lower 2?"

"Ah didn't much notice him, sah. But Ah thinks so, sah. Yes, sah."

"Where did he get on?"

"Now Ah remembers, sah. Ah didn't see him get on, but he came through with the Pullman conductor. He didn't have no ticket, sah. Paid cash to Chicago."

"Why, of all the—!" exploded the young man.

"Shut up!" said the inspector. "You're the person, all right. Will you come along quietly to headquarters, or shall I have to put on the bracelets?"

"But what—what am I supposed to have done?"

"I dunno. The Fargo police wired for us to hold you. You answer the description all right, and the porter's story checks, and yours doesn't. Come along."

Not waiting to hear any more, Deane tiptoed down the corridor and out of the car. Then hurried to the front of the train, so as to be one of the first to get off, and out of the station. Nor did he draw a calm breath until he was safely out on the street.

Once again he bought himself a bag and outfit. And this time a hat. Also had a shave and his suit pressed. Then walked to the Union Station and took a night train to New York. The train finally pulled out of the station, without any further untoward occurrences.

HE HAD THOUGHT of taking the night mail-plane, but gave that up as being too conspicuous. He had thought of going by bus, on the idea that his enemies would not expect

him to use such a slow method of transportation; but then
he reflected that its very slowness would give Maitland
time to discover the identity of the dead body in the plane
and receive a report from his scouts in Fargo. So Deane
compromised on a fast train.

The first part of the trip was uneventful. So much so, in
fact, that Deane relaxed to some extent the vigilance and
seclusion which he had displayed en route from Fargo to
Chicago. He even went into the observation car to read.

He was engrossed with a story in one of the popular
magazines when he experienced an uncanny feeling of
being watched. He glanced up, and sure enough a dark
foreign-looking black-bearded man—a Hindu, apparently—was regarding him intently from just across the
aisle. Surprised in his scrutiny, the Hindu at once buried
himself in his own magazine. So also did Deane.

And then there ensued a sort of hide and seek, each
trying to spy on the other when the other was not spying
on him. But suddenly realizing that this game was making
himself conspicuous and was well calculated to confirm
whatever suspicions the Hindu might have of him, Deane
stopped his peeking and paid strict attention to his book
for at least half an hour.

And when at length he did venture to glance up again,
he was relieved to find that the Hindu had relaxed back in
his chair and was sound asleep. Taking advantage of this
situation, Deane studied the man intently, for the purpose
of memorizing his features against a future meeting.

But, to his horror, he immediately noticed something
which completely diverted his attention from this study.
The man was not breathing! There was not the most infin-

itesimal rise and fall of the man's chest, nor the least flicker of hair or beard or mustache in line with the man's nostrils!

Deane's memory flashed back to the time when he had found John Cortlandt Maitland in exactly that same condition on the couch in Maitland's study in New York.

Then, this Hindu too was a member of the sinister secret society who called themselves "The Immortals." Thank God the man was asleep, and pray Heaven that he would stay that way until Deane could get off the train!

At the moment the observation car was vacant except for the two of them. Tiptoeing out of the car, Deane got a timetable and sat down in the washroom of the next car to study it. He found that the next stop would be in twenty minutes. Here, then, he would get off without even going back to his own car for his hat and bag. Thus he would delay the discovery that he had left the train.

He nervously awaited the stop. At last it arrived.

But as he reached the station platform he heard one of the passengers ask, "What's all the commotion ahead?"

And another man replied, "An old bird cashed in up in the observation car. They're carrying him out right now."

"In that event," thought Deane, "I'd better stay near the train until I see whether he comes to life here or later."

So he stuck around the steps of the car. From the car ahead there emerged the conductor and the porter—the latter gray with fright—carrying the limp body of the Hindu, which they placed on a baggage truck, with a rolled-up coat under its head. Another porter brought a blanket. The conductor hurried away into a nearby train office. An inquisitive crowd gathered; but Deane kept well on its outskirts and finally mounted the steps of the car, ready to duck inside as soon as the Hindu should come to life.

The clanging of a gong could be heard in the station courtyard, and then two white-coated men arrived, carrying a stretcher. One of them applied a stethoscope to the chest of the Hindu, examined his eyeballs, and then shook his head. The body was lifted onto the stretcher and carted off.

Deane smiled grimly to himself as he pictured the amazement of the ambulance men, when their supposed corpse should come to life and berate them roundly for disturbing its sleep.

"All aboard," shouted the trainmen.

Well, this solved Deane's problem for the present. If the spy was staying here, he himself might just as well continue on to New York.

The train was well on its way again before it dawned on him that the Hindu might be really dead, after all. Later on, however, came the more disturbing thought that, if by any chance the Hindu were *not* dead, he had undoubtedly wired or phoned ahead the information that Deane was aboard this train.

AT HOBOKEN THAT evening a man with dark glasses came very slowly and deliberately through the car. His slowness and deliberation seemed to be gropingly due to defective eyesight; yet somehow Deane got the impression that the man paused overlong as he came abreast of Deane. And although the glasses masked all expression of the man's eyes, his face was turned searchingly toward Deane for a long period.

Deane was becoming increasingly sensitive to espionage.

Or perhaps was merely becoming increasingly suspicious of espionage where none existed.

As he made his way along the platform under the Pennsylvania Station in New York, he saw the same man now facing the outgoing crowd, and apparently arguing with a redcap who was offering to help him. The man turned into the stream of people just behind Deane.

After mounting the stairs Deane glanced back. There was no one with dark glasses behind him; but there was a man without glasses who looked strangely familiar. And this man followed Deane to the taxi stand.

"So that's the game, is it?" said Deane to himself, as he turned abruptly away and went back through the station and out onto the street. The man again followed him and stood beside him at the curb. A taxi drew up. Deane stepped back to let the other man take it, but the other declined with a courteous smile and wave of the hand.

"You were ahead of me," he said. "I'll take this one."

And he turned and walked away toward another taxi, which was just arriving. There was nothing for Deane to do but take the first cab. So he got in and gave the name of a small Lexington Avenue hotel.

The two cabs started. Deane glanced back through the rear-window and saw that the other cab was following him. It followed him for quite a number of blocks.

"Well," thought he, "late at night though it is, if the Immortals are on my trail, the sooner I get to Donna's house, before I get bumped off, the better."

So he leaned forward and told the driver to change to Cairns' address. But the other cab continued to follow, until finally it forged ahead. Then, to Deane's surprise, his cab followed it.

He couldn't very well make a fool of himself by telling his driver not to follow the other cab. But he could ask the driver to go more slowly. A card in the cab stated, "If you wish to go more slowly, ask the driver."

So Deane leaned forward and said, "Would you mind slowing up? I was in an auto accident recently and feel a little nervous."

"Yes, sir," the man replied but kept right on following the other cab.

The card also stated, "Select your own route," so Deane looked out of the window to see where he was, so that he could give proper directions for some other routing to the house of the Cairnses.

AND SUDDENLY HE realized that he was being swiftly taken into the wrong part of the city altogether. His mind flashed back to his eventful taxi ride in Fargo. Regardless of whether his present ride was a repetition of that one, or another attempt at kidnaping by Maitland, he wanted to get out of it.

Both cars had now stopped for a red light. The eyes of Deane's driver were intently on the car ahead. So Deane quietly opened the door, slipped out and, dodging between two parked cars, gained the sidewalk, just then the light changed.

Deane had taken care not to close the door of his cab, lest the sound attract the attention of the driver. Now, as the cab started up, the door swung open, caught on one of the parked cars, and ripped half off.

"Hi, there!" shouted the chauffeur of the parked car.

The taxi-driver turned around at the ripping sound and the chauffeur's shout, and saw Deane escaping.

"Hi, there!" *he* shouted. "Come back here and pay for your ride!"

"And for scratching up my car!" added the parked chauffeur.

Deane heard the whistle of an approaching traffic cop. Not waiting for any more, he ducked into a subway entrance which loomed invitingly near by. It turned out to be an exit, rather than an entrance, but he didn't dare go back. As he reached the bottom, quite a number of people came through the gate, which fortunately was of the swinging variety, and so he was able to wedge his way through.

A northbound train came along. He boarded it. The doors slammed shut. A policeman came running along the platform. But the train started.

Deane doubted that the traffic cop had a very good idea of his appearance, or that the taxi driver had had time to describe him. Certainly, if the driver were one of the Maitland gang, he wouldn't even want to give a correct description. So Deane was probably safe from that quarter.

The problem was now to beat the gang to the house of Donna Cairns. It would take a little time for his driver to inform the man with—or rather now without—the dark glasses, of Deane's change of destination. And, anyway, the subway would beat a taxi uptown.

So Deane stayed on the train, until the station nearest to the Cairnses, and then took a taxi from there.

"Is Miss Donna at home?" he inquired.

"Who is calling?" asked the butler.

What should he say? He ought to have foreseen this obvious question, and been prepared for it. He could not give his own name, the name of the supposed murderer of her father. He could not say "a man with a message from her father," for she would be shocked by the apparent callous levity of such a statement.

"I'm Mr. Horace Jones," said he, with sudden resolution. "She doesn't know me, but I have a very important message for her."

"Very well, sir. Will you come in?" said the butler, showing him into a small reception room off the hall.

Presently Donna Cairns entered, in clinging filmy gown. Deane noted with a pang how changed she was since the night he had met her at his lecture on stratium. She was now thin and wan, and her wistful beauty had taken on an ethereal tone. Her wavy chestnut hair seemed to have lost some of its vitality, and her soft brown eyes had become hollow.

She greeted him tentatively, and he instantly realized with relief that she did not recognize him. This simplified his problem.

"Miss Cairns," said he, "prepare yourself for some startling news. I am a detective who has been working on your father's case."

She gasped and clutched her robe to her chest.

Deane held up one hand as he continued, in what he imagined would be the proper manner for a police inspector, "Now hold onto yourself and please, please don't make a scene. Your father is still alive. We have just discovered that he was kidnaped, not killed; and that another body was substituted for his."

Rigid with a sort of fascinated terror, she watched him unblinking, with a slight though increasing negative shaking of her head as he continued.

"My dear young lady," said he, "I know it sounds preposterous, but I have a letter from him in his own handwriting to prove it."

He ran his left hand triumphantly into the inside breast pocket of his coat.

There was no letter there!

11

IN THE TOILS

"BUT I DID have the letter!" Deane exclaimed. "I must have left it in my other suit."

With dawning recognition and contempt she stared at him. Then she cried:

"I know you now. You are Dr. Deane, the man who killed my father. What do you mean by coming here and taunting me?"

"Miss Cairns," he hurriedly replied, "the only reason that I told you that I was a detective was so as to lead up gently to my message. Your father and I were both kidnaped by the same gang. A dead man resembling him was planted in my laboratory. For sometime we were kept apart, but finally we got together. He gave me the letter, which I have unfortunately mislaid; and I escaped. Please believe me. Your father's safety may depend upon it."

"Oh, I can't stand any more!" she cried, and putting her handkerchief into her mouth, she rushed from the room and up the stairs.

Deane ran after her into the hall, calling after her, "Miss Cairns!"

But she ran on up and disappeared around a turn at the head of the stairs. Deane was in a quandary. He could not very well pursue her into the upper reaches of the house. Ought he leave? She had not told him to.

He ran his fingers through his sandy hair in bewilderment. Then he figured that Donna's failure to tell him to leave gave him a chance to stay, until perhaps she might come down again and permit him to prove the truth of his story. So he returned to the reception room and began to pace nervously up and down.

Five minutes passed. Ten minutes. Then the butler entered, visibly perturbed.

"Miss Donna requests," he announced, "that you should wait here. She will be down very shortly. What you said about her father has upset her mightily. She is having a good cry right now, but as soon as she gets over it she wishes to hear further. So just make yourself at home, sir."

The butler bowed himself out. Deane sat down to wait. Things were not going so badly after all. Even without Cairns's letter he might still be able to convince the old professor's daughter. But he worried about the possibility of Maitland finding the letter in his other suit, back at Sioux Lodge.

Donna came in. Her face was calm again, and all signs of her recent tears had been effaced. She even had a fresh handkerchief. But Deane noticed that the butler remained in the hallway just outside the door.

Taking a seat, she said, "And now, Dr. Deane, you may continue. Please forgive me for my outburst, but you must realize what a shock it was for me to have the supposed murderer"—she paused, gripped her hands together in her lap, and then with an effort continued—"of my father have the apparent effrontery to come to my house and taunt me with a vulgar jest. But go on—I am willing to listen to you."

"Miss Cairns," said Deane with deep feeling, "I don't blame you for a thing. Your reaction was entirely natural. But, thank God, it is over, and you are at last willing to let me explain. For you *must* do so; your father's life may depend on you and me working together."

He paused and looked at her narrowly. For he had suddenly noticed that she seemed to be listening for something.

The doorbell rang. Donna Cairns sighed, unclenched her hands, and the tense look left her face.

"Show them in, Higgins," she called and there was almost a note of triumph in her voice.

Then she turned back to her guest with, "You were saying, Dr. Deane—"

There was a commotion in the hall.

"But, my word!" the butler exclaimed.

Then a rough voice interrupted. "Back over against the wall there! Stick up your hands!"

And three men with drawn automatics barged into the room.

Deane jumped to his feet and pushed Donna to one side.

"So!" said he. "I thought so."

FOR ONE OF the three men was the polite gentleman who had followed him out of the Pennsylvania Station that evening, and the others were the two thugs with whom he had battled in the taxicab on the way to the house of John Cortlandt Maitland on the morning of the supposed murder of Professor Cairns, months ago.

"I suppose," Deane grimly added, "that your skull-faced

chauffeur is the man who is guarding Higgins out in the hall."

"These seem to be old friends of yours. Dr. Deane," said Donna sweetly.

"We take it he's no friend of yours, lady," said the polite gentleman. "So don't you worry. We're after him, not you."

"Oh, I'm not worrying at all," she airily replied. "The fact is, I thought when you rang that you were the police. I had phoned for them to come and get this man for the murder of my father. They ought to be here any minute now."

"The hell you say," exclaimed the leader, losing his suavity. "Here, you, Deane, out the back way with us and be quick about it."

The two thugs pounced upon their captive and hustled him out into the hall while their leader followed, with pistol alert. In the hall, sure enough, it was the skull-faced taxi driver of that mad ride to Maitland's brownstone front, months ago, who now held the butler cornered.

"Come on, Snippy," commanded the leader. "Back away, keep a drop on the butler and cover our retreat. If he or the skirt starts anything, shoot."

"Oh, you needn't worry about me," asserted Donna, appearing at the door of the reception room. "I'm quite happy to have you take Dr. Deane for a ride. It will save the expense, the agony, and the uncertainty of a murder trial."

Deane thought he saw a chance to grab the gun of one of his captors. But Donna was in range, in danger of being hit by a stray bullet. So, for her sake, he gritted his teeth and marched peacefully off with the henchmen of Maitland.

Down the hall they went and out through the servants'

rooms to the rear door. This door opened into a jet dark areaway.

But as they filed out the place was suddenly flooded with light and a sharp command rang out, "Drop your guns! We have you covered!"

It was the police.

"Out of the frying pan into the fire," thought Charles Deane. He had failed to get his mission across before falling into the hands of the authorities. Now his only hope was to convince the district attorney, and his one bit of convincing evidence was missing.

As the police closed in on the four gangsters he stepped boldly forward, and announced, "I'm Dr. Charles Deane; I want to get immediately in touch with District Attorney McGrady. It's of vital importance."

"Oh, we know who you are, all right," sneered the police sergeant in charge. "The little lady phoned headquarters all about you. And Dan McGrady will talk to you when he gets good and ready. Will you come peaceably or do you want the bracelets?"

He heard the mocking laugh of Donna Cairns from inside the kitchen.

"I'll come peaceably," said he grimly.

Then the five captives were marched off to the wagon.

Fortunately for Deane's rest that night, he was locked up in a cell with a total stranger, rather than with any of the four Maitland men. His worries for the safety of Professor Cairns, whose daughter had so impetuously spoiled everything, were disturbing enough, without having to keep on his guard all night watching their enemies. And, speaking of enemies, was Donna herself safe? And even if she were safe, what about her finances, with her father gone?

Finally Deane slept.

EARLY THE NEXT morning he was awakened for breakfast, and then was taken to the identification division for photographing and finger-printing.

Immediately he insisted on an interview with the district attorney. But the policeman promptly refused.

"Why?" urged Deane.

"Because, McGrady is off this case."

"But why?"

"Search me. Those are our instructions."

"Mighty strange, don't you think? A double murder, and the D.A. lets a subordinate handle it!"

"Search me! But it's lucky for you, young fellow, that you aren't up against Dan in person."

"I wonder," said Deane.

He submitted to the snapping of a front and a profile view, with a serial number pinned to his chest and shoulders.

But when it came to putting his finger tips on the ink pad he shook his head.

"No, no!" said he.

"Come on! Come on!" badgered the officer. "Every one booked here has to be finger-printed. Who do you think you are, anyhow?"

"I refuse to answer on advice of counsel," Deane replied, grinning.

"Come on! Don't try to horse me!"

"Look here," said Deane sharply. "I'm under indictment for murder. For *two* murders, so far as I know, although I haven't been told. I don't have to give any evidence which might tend to incriminate me. And finger-prints are evidence, aren't they?"

"Say, that's a new one!" exclaimed the officer, with real admiration in his eyes. "It's a wonder that no crook ever thought of *that* line before."

"Isn't it?" Deane assented. "But that's my story, and I'll stick to it."

Only for a moment did the officer's admiration persist. "Here, you!" he exclaimed. "This is all hooey! Everybody that comes in here, gets finger-printed, and you're no exception."

So saying, he grabbed Deane by the wrist, Deane's first reaction was intense resentment at being manhandled. As a matter of fact, his objection to having his finger-prints taken had been merely instinctive rather than based on any particularly reasoned calculations.

Deane jerked his hand away and wheeled about, his fists raised on the defensive. Then, for a moment, the futility of resistance was borne in on him. But only for a moment. For suddenly the thought occurred to him that a rumpus might attract the attention of District Attorney McGrady, which was just what he wanted.

So, with lightning-like speed, he stepped forward and lunged at the policeman.

Down crashed the man, but instantly three others swarmed into the room. A whistle sounded in the corridor outside. Deane, with his back to the wall, fought them off. This was like old college days! The man who ran through the whole Southern California team in the Rose Bowl could hold off four policemen.

And then a keen-looking, red-haired man of apparently about Deane's age appeared in the doorway and cast his blue eyes quickly, and inquiringly around the room. Deane stared hopefully at the newcomer. Was this Dan—?

DEANE CAME TO his senses, alone in a cell—a different cell from the one in which he had formerly been confined. His head ached, and he felt nauseated. Running his fingers tenderly over his scalp, he located a bruised and bloody bump. He inspected his fingers. Mingled with the fresh blood there were traces of ink. Quite evidently he had been finger-printed, after all, and he had not secured an interview with McGrady. All his effort had been for nothing.

He stared around his new quarters. Not only was there no other prisoner to share it, but his keen mind instantly noted another peculiarity, namely a rather large mirror set in the rear wall.

The presence of this mirror intrigued him. Why a mirror in a prison cell? The glass was evidently plate of the best quality; but the silvering, although even, seemed to be unusually dark: more like black night outside the window of a brightly lighted room than like a mirror. Deane vaguely remembered having seen somewhere a mirror like this.

He sat down and delved into his memory, but without results.

A guard arrived, unlocked the barred door, and informed him that his lawyer was waiting to see him in the interview room. His lawyer? He had no lawyer. Wonderingly he followed the guard out to the room with the long table, two benches and the dividing screen, where interviews were permitted. And there, smirking at him on the other side of the wire netting, was the pudgy little Peter Markham, whom he had met at the house of John Cortlandt Maitland.

As Deane took his seat at the long table, the little lawyer shoved his fat white dirty-nailed fingers through the netting and wiggled them at his client. They reminded Deane of loathsome white grubs, black heads and all. He cringed and omitted to grasp them.

Markham withdrew the proffered hand, unabashed, and said ingraciatingly, "Well, you sent for me, and here I am. At your service."

"I did not—Deane indignantly began.

The lawyer held up one hand in protest, and raised his eyebrows meaningfully. Then continued, "It is a good thing that you did send for me. You are in a tough spot."

"Are you in touch with Maitland?" Deane asked pointedly.

"Maitland? You mean John Cortlandt Maitland, the banker? I hardly know the man. No. Why do you ask that?"

There was an amused twinkle in Markham's eyes which belied his words.

"Oh, nothing," Deane lamely replied.

"Anything particular that I could do for you right now?"

"Yes," said Deane suddenly. "Get me a personal interview with the district attorney."

Markham's fat lids narrowed ominously for an instant. Then he pursed his lips and shook his head.

"I advise against it," said he, "You have a much better chance of acquittal if some underling prosecutes you. Let's not attract McGrady's personal attention to your case."

Of course the Maitland gang didn't want him to get in

touch with McGrady, but it was just as well to know it. Deane smiled to himself and changed the subject.

"What makes you think I'm in a tough spot?" he asked.

"It's the finger-prints," Markham replied. "They found your prints on the gun which killed Wolf Diggs, as well as on the knife which stabbed Professor Cairns."

"I think you told me all this once before," said Deane levelly. "And I think that I told you that it was impossible for the authorities to identify my prints. For I have never been finger-printed—that is, not until this morning," he added wryly, lifting his hand and feeling tentatively of his bruised head.

"You have no reason to suppose—?" began Markham, his voice full of ill-concealed concern.

"I have *every* reason to suppose!" Deane cut in. "The chances are that whatever prints of mine they have for comparison are phony. And if the prints on the gun and knife check with these, then they must be phony too."

"Then I tell you what." The lawyer leaned forward close to the wires. "It's important, for your protection, that I get a set of your genuine prints, so as to check up on the phony prints which the Department has. I'll bring around a pad the next time that I come to see you."

Said Deane to himself, "Now I wonder." But aloud he said, "All right."

"Interview over," announced the officer in charge.

And disdaining the again proffered grublike fingers of the lawyer, Deane nodded good-by, and got up and returned to his cell.

IT WAS A dark, overcast day. The lights were turned on. The noon meal was brought. Deane ate slowly and thoughtfully, trying to figure out the reason for Lawyer Markham's intense interest in the matter of finger-prints. Some one had slipped somewhere, and the Maitland gang was just beginning to find it out.

As Deane drained the coffee from his tin cup, the reflection of one of the room lights flickered from the bottom of the cup onto the walls of the room. And suddenly he had an idea.

First he experimented until he had succeeded in capturing the brightest reflection of all; and then he swung the beam over onto the dark wall mirror! And, for an instant, he glimpsed a face in the depths of the mirror! A face whose eyes blinked and whose jaw dropped with an expression of thwarted surprise, ere it faded away in the black depths of the glass!

12

THE FACE IN THE MIRROR

"SO THAT'S THE idea!" said Deane to himself. "Well, I'll be careful of what I do from now on. And of what I say, too," he added, "for doubtless this place is wired with dictaphones as well."

Then he spoke aloud, "If that's you, Mr. District Attorney, I'd like a personal interview with you."

Later that afternoon the district attorney sent for him. On being shown into McGrady's office, Deane took the proffered seat. For a few moments the two men stared at each other, sizing each other up. Yes, the district attorney was the same man who had appeared in the doorway of the finger-print room just before Deane had been knocked cold; the same man whose face Deane had seen through the mysterious mirror in his cell.

"I hear you are ready to talk," said the D.A. briskly.

"Ready to talk!" exploded Deane. "I've been trying to get a chance to talk to you ever since I was arrested. I rather thought I recognized your face."

Ignoring this sally, McGrady snapped, "Well, I'm listening."

"I want to talk to you privately." The district attorney motioned to the policeman to leave, then reached into a

*A fog-like vapor squirted
from the edges of the desk*

desk drawer and ostentatiously produced an automatic
pistol, which he laid on the desk close to his right hand.

"Proceed!" he snapped.

"Are you sure this room isn't wired?" cautioned Deane.

"Well—"

"I thought so," Deane asserted. "Please switch it off. I'm
prepared to talk to you, but not to make a stenographic
confession."

Dan McGrady grinned engagingly.

"You win," said he. "I'll give you my word, as one football
player to another, that the dictaphone is now off."

"Speaking of football," said Deane, grinning back, "I saw
you make that end run for Harvard against Yale in your
senior year, and let me tell you—"

They swapped football yarns for about twenty minutes.

Finally McGrady broke in apologetically with, "I'd
almost forgotten that this is a business conference; not
a college reunion. You're in an awful mess, Deane. Better
come clean."

"O.K.," said the other; and then he gave a succinct account of everything from the time when Wolf Diggs had stumbled out through the door of his Wall Street office, to fall dying at Deane's feet, through all the enmeshing intrigues of the Order of the Immortals, down to his interview with Lawyer Markham that afternoon.

When he finished McGrady dryly remarked, but with a twinkle in his blue Irish eyes, "As Professor Joey Beale used to say at Harvard Law, 'It sounds like the ravings of an opium dream.' And yet somehow I believe that you believe all this fantastic yarn really happened. But how do you explain away the finger-print evidence?"

"It may have been planted," Deane replied with a slight sniff.

"Impossible. The exhibits have been in the constant possession of trusted employees of this Department."

"The finger-prints might have been planted on the exhibits before you got hold of them. Furthermore, your Department has had no genuine prints of mine to compare with."

"That lack was remedied this morning," said the district attorney with a grin. "Though, to tell the truth, you were right on your law; for I've just looked the matter up and find that *People* versus *Stevens*, 215 N.Y.S. 412, is the only case on the subject, and it holds that a suspect has a constitutional right to refuse to be printed. But, fortunately the case isn't mentioned in any of the law books. Think what a godsend it would be to the crooked gang-lawyers if it became known!"

"A lot of good it would do them," Deane wryly remarked, feeling of his bruised head.

"Well," said McGrady, grinning, "let's get going. The clue to this whole situation may rest in your finger-prints." Then pressing a desk-button, he spoke into the microphone on his desk, "Send in Schwartz."

"And who is Schwartz?" Deane asked.

"The identification expert of my Department."

Presently Schwartz was shown in, a bullet-headed fellow, with a Prussian haircut, and thick lenses to his eyeglasses, which concealed his facial expression, if any.

"Schwartz, this is Charles Deane. The Diggs and Cairns cases, you know."

SCHWARTZ TURNED HIS expressionless face toward Deane, then back to his superior again, but made no other acknowledgment of the introduction.

"Vell?" he asked.

"Schwartz," said the D.A., "what did you use to check the finger-prints found on the Diggs revolver and the Cairns knife?"

"Vell, ve yoost prints vitch ve took from der laboratory. A plenty."

"Have you checked them with the prints which were taken this morning?"

"No. Nod yet. Vy?"

An expression of furtive fear flickered across the man's face for an instant.

"Oh, nothing," McGrady disarmingly replied, and then began to ask questions about the exhibits in the case.

As McGrady continued his interrogation of Schwartz, Deane watched him intently. Something about the man suggested a clue. What was it?

And then Deane almost gasped with recognition, as he

realized that Schwartz was breathing only when respond-
ing to questions. During the rest of the time his huge barrel
chest remained absolutely quiet. Deane smiled grimly to
himself.

Finally McGrady dismissed the expert. As Schwartz
rose to go, Deane rose too, and advanced with hand
outstretched as though to say good-by. Then suddenly,
without warning, flung himself on Schwartz.

"You dirty crook!" he screamed. "You would frame me,
would you?" And seizing the surprised Schwartz by the
wrists, he dug his nails into the man's arms. Schwartz
wrenched one hand free and lunged at his assailant. Deane
recoiled from the blow and staggered back across the room.

By this time McGrady was on his feet, with the automatic in his hand. "Stand back there, Deane!" he shouted.
"Stand back, or I'll drill you!"

Deane shrugged his shoulders with a gesture of resignation; and sinking into a chair, wiped the blood from his
finger tips with his pocket handkerchief and then stuffed
it back into his pocket.

Two burly cops entered on the run.

"Seize the prisoner!" McGrady commanded. Then rushing over to the spluttering German, he mopped the man's
red and dripping wrists with an apologetic, "I'm sorry,
Schwartz. It's my fault entirely, for permitting a desperate
murderer to be unguarded like this. You'd better see the
prison surgeon at once. Have you a clean handkerchief?"

Throwing his own handkerchief, red and dripping, into
a wastebasket, he took Schwartz's, tore it in half, and deftly
bandaged the two lacerated wrists.

Then the German, his round face knotted with perplexed rage, departed, muttering, *"Dummkopf! Schzveinhund!"*

McGrady turned toward Deane, where he stood firmly held in the grip of the two policemen.

"So? So you showed the sort of fellow you really are?" he sneered. "All right, men, let go of him, step outside the door and remain within call. This fellow is just about ripe for a confession if I handle him alone."

"But, chief—" one of the officers started to object.

"Don't worry about *me*," asserted McGrady, twirling his automatic on his forefinger. "This fellow knows a gat when he sees one."

So the two cops reluctantly withdrew.

AS THEY CLOSED the door the expression on McGrady's Irish face changed from truculence to amused concern. He winked broadly at his prisoner and beckoned with one finger. Perplexed, Deane drew near the district attorney's desk.

Then McGrady spoke in a low tone, "I'm not altogether an idiot, Deane. You put on a good act, and it fooled Schwartz completely, but it didn't fool me. What caused you to suspect him?"

A relieved grin spread over Deane's face as he replied, "I noticed that he didn't breathe at all except when he was talking to you."

"Well, let's see if you are right."

McGrady gingerly fished his own blood-soaked handkerchief out of the wastebasket and held it close to his nose.

"Um! It *does* smell like hydrogen peroxide."

"And it's still bright crimson, instead of turning brown," Deane added.

"You win!" asserted the district attorney, with appreciation twinkling in his blue Irish eyes, as he wrapped the tell-tale rag in a piece of newspaper and stuffed it in a drawer of his desk. "Well, where do we go from here?"

"It seems to me," said his prisoner thoughtfully, "that there's at least an even chance that Schwartz has slipped, and has forged the finger-prints of my laboratory assistant, Angus Frazer, on the exhibits, instead of mine."

"So? You'll be free in five minutes; if that's the case," said McGrady, reaching for the desk-button.

But Deane halted him with, "Stop! I'm not interested in getting myself off. What I want to do is catch the gang. Do you understand finger-print classification?"

"Somewhat. Yes, I should say yes."

"Well, then, let's get hold of the prints which Schwartz is using as mine. And also of the prints which they took of Angus Frazer when they arrested him for complicity in the Cairns murder. Of course Schwartz mustn't know that we are doing this."

"Of course not," thoughtfully. "Yes, I believe I can rummage through his files right now. He's probably gone home."

EARLY THE NEXT morning District Attorney McGrady sent for the prisoner again. As soon as Deane was seated, and the officer who had brought him had left the room, the D.A. said:

"I'm beginning to believe your entire story. Of course, I'm no finger-print expert, but Frazer's card and your alleged card are identical so far as I can see. At least they have exactly the same classification number. It's a wonder that Schwartz didn't tumble to that. I've left them side by side in his file, in the hopes that he will."

"But why—?" Deane started to expostulate. Then, with sudden comprehension, "Oh, I see. Now all we've got to do is watch Schwartz make a new forgery, now that he has some *genuine* prints of mine to compare with."

"And Schwartz took your genuine prints home with him last night," added MeGrady. "He's probably in his laboratory right now. Let's see what he is doing. Come on!"

So saying, he stepped over to the wall and pushed a hidden spring, causing one of the panels to slide open. Beckoning to Deane, he stepped inside. Deane followed. The panel swung closed, leaving the two men in absolute darkness.

"The X-ray corridor, so called," MeGrady explained, in a whisper. "You spotted the X-ray mirror in your cell, when I was spying on you. But what Schwartz doesn't know is that the mirror over the washstand in his laboratory is transparent too. Come on, follow me. Keep quiet. And don't stumble."

In single file the two men threaded the dark and winding passageway. At last they reached some plumbing pipes, above which there stood in the wall a rectangular niche, which glowed faintly with a silver luminescence. And, when they stood abreast of it, they were able to see right through into a brightly lighted room. There at a work bench, facing them, sat Schwartz; and spread on the bench before him were the exhibits in the case of *The People of the State of New York* versus *Charles Deane.*

It seemed almost incredible that Schwartz could not see the two watchers as clearly as they could see him; and yet

Deane knew, from his experience with X-ray mirrors, that so long as he stood a foot or two back from the niche he was absolutely safe from detection.

On the table in front of the big German were an automatic pistol, a laboratory knife, a number of photographs and several finger-print charts.

From one of his pockets Schwartz took ten rubber finger-cots. One by one he placed them on his own fingers, touched them to an ink pad, printed them on a clean piece of paper, and then compared the results with one of the charts.

When each cot had been finally identified and placed on its proper finger, Schwartz made a print of all five finger-prints of each hand and compared that with the master chart. Then made some adjustments, including stuffing two of the cots with a small quantity of crumpled paper.

Finally all was in shape to his satisfaction. He got up, and came over to the sink. McGrady and Deane backed away from the niche until Schwartz had finished washing off the ink and had returned to his bench.

Schwartz rubbed the finger-cots one by one on the side of his nose. Then, picking up the gun by the muzzle with his left hand, he grasped the stock with his right and slid the slide back with his left; then pulled the trigger. The hammer clicked into place.

Carefully laying down the firearm, he again rubbed his nose and picked up the knife.

These preliminaries over, he removed the finger-cots, shoved them in his pocket, dusted powder on the two exhibits and took photographs of them from many angles. The case of *The People* against *Charles Deane* was complete.

13

THE STATE STRIKES

THE CEREMONIES WERE concluded by Schwartz burning, in his laboratory furnace, all the old photographs, the old supposed set of Deane's finger-prints, and all his own test-sheets.

The case of *The People* against *Schwartz* was now complete. District Attorney McGrady led the way back through the dark passage to his own office.

"Well," asked Deane, when they were back in the lighted room once more, "what do you propose to do now?"

"Swear out a John Doe warrant for the murderer of Wolf Diggs and Oscar Cairns," snapped the D.A.

"And who is John Doe?"

"His name is John, all right. John Cortlandt Maitland!"

"But Cairns isn't dead, you know," Deane reminded him.

"I don't know it yet *officially*," McGrady retorted, "so I might as well have two strings to my bow."

He pushed a desk button, and spoke into the microphone, "Send for Inspector Lally."

When that official reported, McGrady snapped out the order, "Have operatives trail Schwartz and Lawyer Peter Markham. Keep me posted as to every move of the two suspects, especially if they meet."

"What Schwartz, sir?"

"Our own Schwartz. Schwartz, the identification expert. And be sure that all the operatives on both cases are men whom Schwartz won't recognize."

When Lally had withdrawn, McGrady took some blank forms from a filing cabinet.

"And now," said he, "to fill out a very necessary paper."

Something in his tone, and in the twinkle of his blue eyes, caused Deane to ask, "What paper?"

"A nolle prosequi of the charges against one Charles Deane," was the reply.

"And would you please include Angus Frazer?"

McGrady shook his red head, then grinned engagingly.

"I'm a poor overworked, underpaid public official," said he. "Now I'll have to get up again and walk all the way over to that filing cabinet and get out a blank for your friend."

When the second nolle prosequi had been made out Deane said, "Not that I like living in jail, but don't you think it would be advisable not to free me yet?"

"You're quite right," commented McGrady soberly. "If an old-timer like Schwartz is a two-timer, who can we trust?"

"But," continued Deane, "there is one person whom I would like to have know that I'm innocent; and that is Donna Cairns."

"Daughter of Professor Cairns?"

"Yes."

"I'll send for her."

"Gosh," said Deane admiringly, "it must be nice to be able to order girls around like that."

"It's a gift," McGrady airily replied.

So the District Attorney phoned and made arrangements, and sent a squad car over for Donna Cairns.

She came graciously and inquiringly into the office; then, when she saw that Deane was there, she raised one hand to her mouth.

"Oh, Mr. McGrady," she gasped, "this is much too much."

"But my dear Miss Cairns," said the D.A., "your father is still alive. Mr. Deane and your father were both kidnaped by the same gang. Mr. Deane escaped at great risk of his own life, came to New York at all kinds of peril just so as to get in touch with you and secure your help, and was almost kidnaped again right in your own house. And then what do you do, I ask you? You turn him over to the police, and thus waste three valuable days, which might have been spent running down the kidnapers!"

Donna Cairns flared up, and her brown eyes snapped. "So you believe his story," she cried. "What proof has he?"

McGRADY RESTED HIS chin on his left hand, cocked his head on one side, and stared at the girl appraisingly for a full minute before he answered, "You know, you look very beautiful when you're angry, Miss Cairns.

She hung her head and colored prettily.

"Score one for the defense," McGrady chortled. "Now let's get down to business. I have ample proof that Mr. Deane here is telling the truth, and that your father is still alive—or was a week ago."

Hope flooded her face, to be followed by a look of fear.

"You don't mean—" she began, with her hand to her mouth.

"I mean," said the District Attorney, with brutal directness, "that your stupid interference may have made it too late for us to save your father."

"Oh, Dr. Deane," she cried, turning toward him, "how can you ever forgive me?"

"Donna—I mean Miss Cairns," said he, embarrassedly running a hand through his sandy hair, "it certainly is decent of you to think of me and my feelings at a time like this. But never mind me. We've got to save your father."

"First, let's tell her all that we know," interjected McGrady briskly. "Perhaps she can fill in some details. Besides, it won't do any harm for me to review the facts. They aren't any too clear to me, and when you told them to me before I didn't more than half believe you myself. So you see. Miss Cairns," turning to her, "you were not alone in your incredulity."

So Charles Deane once again went through an account of his adventures: the death of Wolf Diggs, the bearded face that had haunted his laboratory, the lecture at which he had announced the discovery of the lighter-than-air metal stratium, the finding of the supposed body of Cairns, the fight in the taxicab, his "rescue" by John Cortlandt Maitland, Sioux Lodge and its paradoxical stratosphere mining, his discovery there of Oscar Cairns still alive, and his flight eastward against the interference of Maitland's gang.

But he did not stress too heavily the presence of the steel-blond Mavis in the picture. When he reached the very recent encounter with Schwartz, the District Attorney drew the "bloody" handkerchief from his desk drawer. It no longer smelled of hydrogen peroxide, but it still was as brilliantly crimson as when it had first mopped Schwartz's wounds.

"We'll have to have this analyzed chemically," McGrady asserted. Then added with a grin, "But not by our friend Schwartz."

Just then the phone rang, and the District Attorney answered it. "So?" he commented. "So?—So?"

Then, hanging up the receiver, he reported, "Both Schwartz and Lawyer Markham have been traced to number ——, Riverside Drive."

"Why, that's Maitland's house!" Deane exclaimed.

"Naturally! What did you expect?" said McGrady. Then pressing a button and speaking into the desk microphone, he commanded, "I want Inspector Lally at once and a strong-arm squad. Also my car. Also a car to take Miss Cairns home. Come on, Deane, I think we are going somewhere, and getting somewhere."

Donna Cairns shook hands good-by with both young men.

Deane held her hand for a moment, as she sought to release it, and murmured to her, "Donna—"

But she shook her head and pulled her hand gently away.

"Please," said she. "I know I oughtn't to feel that way about you, but it still makes me cringe to touch you. I hope to get over it, though."

Then she left.

"I could get interested in that girl," said McGrady.

"Don't get too interested," Deane replied.

"So?" asked the other, raising his eyebrows. "Now, you know, I rather thought that you had intentions on Mavis Maitland. Well, come along. Let's call on Mavis's poppa."

Armed with a search warrant, and accompanied by Inspector Lally and a squad of policemen, they set out for number —— Riverside Drive.

LALLY PLACED MOST of his men in strategic positions, and then he, McGrady, Deane and three men in uniform mounted the broad steps to the brownstone front, and rang the bell.

The butler answered the door.

"Is your master in, Busby?" Deane inquired.

"Shall I sye Mr. 'Orace Jones?" the butler replied, recognizing him.

"Yes, that name'll do as well as any other. Mr. Horace Jones, and five friends."

"Werry well, sir." And he led them into the high hallway, took their hats, and then went away through the tall folding doors of Maitland's study.

Presently he returned and announced, "The marster will see you. This wye, gentlemen."

As they entered, Maitland was sitting behind his desk, with his elbows on the desk, the tips of his fingers together, and the ends of his thumbs resting against his lips. Without rising he gestured first to the right, and then to the left, indicating for them to be seated.

A quizzical smile played upon his bronzed features.

"Ah, my old friend: Dr. Charles Deane," said he, with a trace of a sneer so slight as not to destroy the complete gentlemanliness of his tone. "I see, Doctor, that you prefer the company of the New York police to that of me and my associates at Sioux Lodge. Or perhaps you are planning to return with me. My hospitality is still open to you. Oh, and by the way, my daughter Mavis sent her regards, just in case I should happen to see you, though I hardly expected to."

Deane flushed, and Dan McGrady flashed a grin at him.

Assuming now a more businesslike tone, Maitland suavely continued, "And now, Dr. Deane, please introduce your friends—or should I say 'captors?'"

"You really shouldn't," interjected the District Attorney, "for Dr. Deane has just been completely exonerated from the two murders with which he has been charged."

"Splendid! Splendid!" asserted Maitland, smiling genially. "I always felt that he was innocent. Doubtless he has told you that it was on that assumption that I harbored him. And now mayn't I ring for whiskies and sodas all round, to celebrate the happy deliverance of our friend?"

The policemen looked hopeful, but McGrady held up his hand.

"Thank you, no," said he. "This is purely a business, visit, and business and whisky don't mix."

"Well, have it your own way," said Maitland. "I take it that you are the famous Dan McGrady, New York's youngest and ablest District Attorney. And these others?"

"Inspector Lally and three members of the force."

"Really? And the object of your visit?"

"To place you under arrest for the murder of Wolf Diggs."

"And—"

"And of Oscar Cairns."

A momentary expression of relief flitted across the face of John Cortlandt Maitland, to be instantly succeeded by his usual inscrutability.

McGrady caught it and smiled.

"Please, pardon my inquisitiveness," said Maitland, "but what makes you think that I had anything to do with either of those two crimes?"

"Do I have to answer?" bantered the District Attorney.

"No. Nor, for that matter, do I have to submit to arrest. You ought to know, as a lawyer, McGrady, that the Supreme Court has recently held that an invitation to enter a man's house is revocable, if it is used to make a search or to serve a warrant."

"Who told you that? Peter Markham?"

"Yes. And he also told me that two of your operatives followed him here. Really, McGrady, you ought to keep them under better cover than that. But I'm glad to have you here—really I am—for as long as you are here, I know exactly where you are. And, furthermore, I wanted to find out how much you thought you knew."

"Just what do you mean by that crack?"

McGrady began to show irritation.

"I'll tell you," said Maitland, jumping to his feet, and for once dropping the mask of his suavity. "In the first place, you're not going to arrest me at all. Not while I have—er—legal protection with the police. And now before I go—er—I wish to have a word with my young friend Deane here."

"In private?" asked Deane, surprised.

Maitland shrugged. "No," said he.

"What I have to tell you might just as well be said in the presence of these gentlemen. Deane, I liked you. In fact, I still like you, in spite of your having run out on me. You are an able scientist and a keen and resourceful young man. I need you in my organization. My daughter Mavis likes you, too. She particularly asked me to urge you to come back to us. If I could guarantee you safe passage from this room—would you come with me?"

DEANE WAVERED. HIS mind flashed back to a moonlit hillside in North Dakota, with a lithe and fragrant girlish figure clasped tight in his arms. And to a brave little aviatrix, battling to get him to the landing field in safety ahead of the black plane of the minions of her father. Mavis called to him from across the continent.

"Can you guarantee my safe passage from this room?" he queried.

"Yes," Maitland briskly answered. "You know me well enough by now to know that I always make good my promises—and my threats."

"Not always," said Deane. He was beginning to get a hold on himself again. The moonlit vision was fading.

"Always—in time," asserted Maitland. "And remember that time is the one thing of which I have unlimited quantities."

Dan McGrady jumped to his feet, an automatic in his hand.

"Sit down, Maitland!" he commanded.

But Maitland completely ignored him.

"You'll come, Dr. Deane?" he asked with a note almost of entreaty in his tone.

"No," said Deane firmly. "I'm sorry, sir."

"Mavis will be sorry, too," said Maitland. "Well, on your own head be it. The place is open, any time you choose to change your mind. Good-by, gentlemen."

Suddenly he dropped behind the desk. Dan McGrady fired; the shot struck the top of the desk and glanced harmlessly off. He fired again, squarely at the desk, but the bullet did not penetrate. He leaped forward with raised pistol in hand; and then staggered back, as a blast of fog-like vapor squirted at him from the edges of the desk.

Deane too leaped forward, and was similarly hurled back. The room filled with vapor from all sides. Deane and McGrady dropped to their knees. All around them, their four companions were writhing on the floor.

Maitland arose from behind the desk, a triumphant smile on his bronzed face.

"There is still a chance, Deane," said he. "I don't have to breathe, you know, so I can get you out."

Deane shook his head, and then pitched forward on his face. His head swam and he seemed to lose consciousness.

Then for a moment his head cleared again. Looking up, he saw Maitland and Schwartz and Markham undressing the three policemen.

14

THE SIEGE

THE NEXT THING that Charles Deane knew, some one was shaking him. He opened his eyes and looked around. He was still lying on the floor of Maitland's study. A policeman and a man in a white ambulance coat were bending over him.

"He's coming round," said the man in white.

"Damn it," said the voice of Dan McGrady near by. "Did you let them make a complete get-away?"

"We've searched the entire house," said another voice apologetically, "and there's not a soul here."

"Tell me just what happened," McGrady demanded.

"Well," said the other, "three policemen came out of the house—one of them was Schwartz from Headquarters. They had the butler with them, handcuffed. Schwartz said that your orders were to keep out of the house, and let you handle it. So—"

"Three policemen!" snorted McGrady. "One of them was Maitland, and one was his crooked lawyer, Markham. And Schwartz is a member of their gang."

"How were we to know? Well, anyway, after a long time and nothing happening, we got suspicious. So we broke in, and here we are."

"They got away in a squad car? Let me to the telephone."

He staggered to his feet, lurched over to the desk, and dialed Police Headquarters. Then waited. But no one answered. So he replaced the receiver. Then took it off again, and waited for the dial tone. But no dial tone came.

"Line dead," he succinctly announced. "Wires cut. Beat it out to the nearest phone, one of you, and notify Headquarters to radio all cars to stop the squad car that Maitland is in. I'm too weak to make it."

He slouched in his chair and gasped for breath.

Gradually Deane's head cleared, and he got up off the floor and joined McGrady.

"You two ought to go to bed and rest up," cautioned the white-coated physician solicitously. "You've been badly gassed."

"Bed, hell!" retorted McGrady.

"This is war."

He shook his head with a little shudder, and wrinkled up his nose. Deane ran his fingers through his hair and stretched the muscles of his face; then drew a deep breath.

"Let's get going," said he.

"Back to my office, then," declared McGrady. "We'll direct the campaign from there."

So, with sirens shrieking, they sped back to Police Headquarters.

Scarcely were they back in the District Attorney's office when a buzzer rang, and the desk phone spoke. "Miss Donna Cairns abducted from her home. We are holding her butler."

The two men stared at each other for a moment in horror.

Then, "I'm going there," Deane declared.

"You know how much I wish I could go, too, old fellow," said McGrady, with deep concern in his voice. "I'll put a car and a couple of cops at your disposal."

And he gave the necessary instructions into the microphone.

In spite of Deane's worry over Donna's fate, he could not help exulting as he walked out of Police Headquarters under his own power. He was free, free again for the first time since he had fled from his laboratory that morning over three months ago, after finding the dead body which he had supposed to be that of Professor Cairns. Now no longer was he a fugitive from either the authorities or the Immortals, nor was he any longer a prisoner of either. He was free, free!

But Donna Cairns was not free. She was a prisoner of the same sinister forces which had held him. Which still held her father and Angus Frazer. The thought sobered him, and cooled his momentary exultation.

On Deane's arrival at the Cairns residence he did not learn much. Four men had forced their way into the house, had bound and gagged the butler, and had bound and gagged Miss Donna and carried her away. The butler was unable to describe his assailants.

THE POLICE, HOWEVER, had combed the neighborhood, and had gotten a fairly good description of the kidnap car from some small boys who had been playing in the alley where it was parked. This description was now being broadcast.

Deane phoned McGrady.

"Got 'em both!" was the reply.

"What! Who? Donna and Maitland?"

"No. I wish it were. What I mean is that both autos—the squad car which Maitland stole from us, and the car which carried Don—I mean, Miss Cairns—have been traced to the water front warehouse of Simpson Brothers, a Maitland subsidiary. The place is surrounded. They can't escape. Meet you there."

So Deane and his bodyguard sped to the designated rendezvous. Dan McGrady was already there ahead of him, handing out olive-drab canvas knapsacks about ten inches square.

"Gas masks," he explained as Deane got out of his car. "The ambulance surgeon took a sample of the gas from Maitland's library, and rushed it up to Columbia, where they did a quick job of analysis for us. Luckily it's a simple chemical, already provided for by the contents of the standard canister. So we're as immortal as the next fellow, for the present."

He handed one of the satchels and an automatic to Deane, and continued, "All right, come on. We're all set."

Locksmiths had been working on the doors and had finally mastered the locks, but still the doors would not open. Doubtless secured in some manner on the inside. All the windows were heavily barred, but acetylene torches soon removed these obstructions; and the wire-glass was battered through. The besiegers were prepared to enter.

Leaving a sufficient force outside to keep the warehouse securely surrounded, a picked squad, armed with 17-shot 45-caliber Michal hand machine guns, crawled in through the smashed window, and began a careful foot-by-foot search of every floor. And with them went McGrady and

Deane. But there appeared to be not a soul in the entire huge structure.

It was Deane who found the first clew: a small lace-edged linen handkerchief, with the initials "D.C." Doubtless she had dropped it in the hope of its being found.

"Good girl!" mused McGrady, when Deane showed it to him. "Well, at least we've traced her this far."

A shout from one of the cops announced, "There's some one in the basement. I hear an automobile-exhaust down there."

And every one piled downstairs. A heavy sliding fire-door barred their way to the basement. Behind it could be heard the "putt-putt-putt" of an exhaust. But the door defied their efforts.

The acetylene torches were brought, and easily burned through the outer steel layer of the door, but then met some composition substance which defied them.

Bring dynamite," barked McGrady.

There was some delay at this, and meanwhile the "putt-putt-putt" died away in a bubbling gurgle, and all was silent below stairs.

BUT AT LAST the dynamite came and was tamped against the door, covered with a pile of wooden beams. The fuses were lit, and every one withdrew to a safe distance.

A crashing roar, and every one rushed forward again, with the flash light beams from their machine guns penetrating the gloom of the yawning chasm caused by the explosion.

But a fine mist was wafted out through the opening, and the first policeman to reach it dropped his weapon, clutched at his chest, and slumped to the concrete floor.

"Gas! One—"barked McGrady.

And, with the precision born of long experience, each member of the invading party laid down his gun, knocked his cap backward off his head with his left hand, at the same instant reaching with his right hand into the satchel which hung on his chest and hauling out a mask.

"Two!"

The masks were shoved up and back over the protruding chins.

"Three!" came the muffled command.

The straps were adjusted.

"Four!"

The squad picked up their guns again, and stood at attention. Deane was still struggling with his unfamiliar mask. McGrady stepped over to him and helped him with it.

Then, "Fine work, boys!" exclaimed the D.A. in a muffled tone.

"Forward—march!"

And—looking like a cross between Micky Mice and elephants—the weird group plunged into the opening.

Through the swirling mist their flash lights disclosed a low damp room with a long wide tank, like a swimming pool in the center, with its farther end butting up against the farther wall of the room. At the near end of the tank stood a man, with an automatic in his hand. He wore no gas-mask and he was not breathing.

All the flash light beams converged upon him. He was John Cortlandt Maitland.

"Drop your gun," grunted McGrady. "We've got you covered."

With a contemptuous gesture Maitland tossed his weapon over his shoulder. It fell with a hollow resounding splash into the pool.

As the echoes died away, McGrady commanded, "Stick up your hands!"

Slowly, very slowly, Maitland obeyed. The District Attorney signaled to one of the policemen to seize the prisoner.

The designated officer laid down his gun and stepped forward with manacles in his hands. But, as be reached up to snap the bracelets on one of Maitland's upraised wrists, the banker suddenly side-stepped so as to place the policeman between himself and the ring of menacing weapons; then hooked one arm around the neck of the man and toppled backward into the pool.

"Brrrrp!" barked one of the guns.

Then every one rushed forward to the water's edge. All lights were turned on the center of the widening eddies. All guns were held alert for the reappearance of Maitland. But he did not reappear!

A stream of bubbles arose. Then a dark blotched stain, which spread with the widening eddies. But still no Maitland.

With sudden determination Charles Deane fled from the scene, found a tumbler in a washroom that he had remembered, rushed back again, and dipped up a sample of the bloody water.

BUT STILL NO sign of either Maitland or the missing policeman. McGrady, signaling to two men to remain and guard the pool, led the rest out of the cellar and removed his gas-mask.

"Gee, but it's good to be out in the fresh air again!" he

ejaculated. "Now what do you suppose Maitland staged that grand-stand play for?"

"Probably so as to hold us off as long as possible, until the rest of his gang made their get-away," Deane ventured.

"More likely just mere spectacular bravado," asserted McGrady. "He always did things in a grand way."

"What I don't see is how he got Donna out of here," mused Deane. "He and the rest of his gang could probably stay under water without breathing, just the same as they go through poison gas. But Donna couldn't. Either they've drowned her, or else she's still in this building."

McGrady sent rush orders for a diver, and meanwhile the search of the warehouse was resumed.

They found no one. But by the side of the basement pool, one of the men picked up several bobbie-pins. Quite evidently Donna Cairns was taking care to leave a paper-trail behind her.

Finally the diver arrived. Electric fans were brought, and dispelled the gas. The diver put on his helmet and descended into the water. Many yards of air-pipe and rope were paid out—much more than the size of the pool could possibly justify. The trail of bubbles from the diver's helmet led to the farther wall, clustered there for quite a while, and then ceased.

At length they reappeared again and then the diver emerged, bearing in his arms the dead body of the missing policeman.

Unscrewing his head-dress, he announced, "There is a wide tunnel leading out into the harbor. But no man could have lived and gone that way."

"They must have taken Donna with them," asserted McGrady soberly.

"But how?" asked Deane.

"Dead!" said McGrady lugubriously.

A pause for a few minutes. Then Deane's face lighted with sudden joy.

"The putt-putt-putt!" he cried. "The motor-exhaust! They must have had a submarine. Donna is safe!"

"I wish I felt as sure of it as you do," soberly replied the District Attorney. "And if so, where are they bound?"

"I have it!" exclaimed Deane. "The Newark airport. Why didn't we think of that before? Come on!"

And he raced upstairs to the nearest phone.

But the phone was dead. The wires here too had been cut.

They found another phone several blocks away. But all the lines to the airport were busy. They all stayed busy.

"Confederates are holding the wires on us," asserted McGrady. "We've got the right hunch."

And he called the Newark police.

But they were too late. The Newark officials reported that Maitland's private plane had taken off with ten passengers including two persons in the uniform of the New York police, and one person on a stretcher.

"Well, anyway, Maitland is hit," Deane commented, "and quite badly hit, I should say. The two supposed policemen would be Schwartz and Markham. Maitland must be the man on the stretcher. But where is Donna? Are you quite sure there was no woman along?"

McGrady repeated the question over the phone.

"No," said he. "They say no women. Well, I hope we've

got Maitland. Let's come back to my office. I want to radio to all airports, and send a detachment of North Dakota police up to Sioux Lodge as a little reception committee."

"But where is Donna?" Deane repeated.

BACK AT POLICE HEADQUARTERS again, the necessary messages were sent out. Deane was installed in Schwartz's laboratory and analyzed the blood sample which he had taken from the waters of the submarine lock. But it proved to be merely human blood. Not a trace of the peculiar-smelling substance which he had learned to identify as the synthetic blood of the Immortals. An autopsy on the drowned policeman showed that he had been struck by two of the burst of bullets meant for Maitland; and a precipitin test indicated that the blood of the policeman and Deane's sample fell in the same one of the four classifications.

But still this didn't prove that Maitland had not been wounded. The fact of the person on the stretcher, clearly led to the conclusion that he or some member of his gang had been pretty badly hit, and he was the only one of them who had been fired at.

No word of Maitland's plane was received during the day from any airport. Deane spent the night at Dan McGrady's bachelor apartment.

Early the next morning the North Dakota police reported that they had been unable to locate Sioux Lodge from the description given them.

"Well," McGrady wryly remarked, "perhaps I'm trying to make sunbeams out of cucumbers, but it may be just as well to let them land, and then close in on them."

And he wired to North Dakota, "Use airplanes in your

search for Sioux Lodge. Spare no expense, and charge to my Department."

Two days later, Sioux Lodge was finally located. But it was deserted. The stratium warehouses and laboratories were empty. The smelters had been dismantled. The stratosphere balloon and all the airplanes were gone. The local labor had been laid off with a fat bonus, and without explanation. No one thereabouts had seen anything moved.

Maitland had been good pay, and the mountaineers were disinclined to talk.

There was, however, a small quantity of the stratium left; and Deane arranged to have this shipped to him in New York, for further experimentation.

From all over the country came reports of Maitland's plane. It had been sighted in almost every state of the Union, going in almost every conceivable direction.

Meanwhile all of the members of Maitland's New York banking office, and even the officials of concerns remotely controlled by him, had been put upon the grill. But nothing was learned, except that for many weeks the master-mind had been liquidating his holdings. But what he had done with all the proceeds, could not be traced.

Only one item of interest developed during this entire period, namely as follows. A further interrogating of everyone who had been at the Newark airport, when the Maitland ship had taken off, had developed the fact that the sex of the invalid on the stretcher was not certain. It *might* have been a woman!

15

A NEW NAPOLEON

THE WEEKS WORE on. No further word from Maitland. He and his gang seemed to have vanished into thin air. The gods had returned to Mount Olympus.

The tracing of his huge fortune continued. But inevitably the trail of each item led to some foreign country, into the hands of some bank or individual who refused to talk.

"This means something, if we could only fathom it," asserted District Attorney McGrady. "Now just why did he liquidate his holdings, and send all his money abroad?"

"Possibly merely to keep the American police off the trail," Deane replied.

"No, it means more than that. I'm sure. And if we could find the answer to that, we'd have the key to the objects of his whole organization. For, like you, I believe that Maitland's aiming at something bigger and grander than has yet been indicated by his American operations."

"True," Deane agreed. "John Cortlandt Maitland never yet did anything on a petty scale."

He had been permanently attached to the staff of the District Attorney, in the position vacated by the fugitive Schwartz. And in his spare time he continued his experiments with the lighter-than-air metal stratium. He had to keep busy, to work himself to exhaustion, in order to keep his mind off worrying as to what had become of Donna Cairns.

"You know, Dan," he said one day to his superior, "I wish that I had taken up Maitland's offer that day just before he gassed us. Then perhaps I would be able to help Donna. At least I would know what had become of her."

"And how would Mavis Maitland have liked that?" McGrady maliciously replied.

Deane flushed. "Oh, Mavis doesn't care anything about me," said he rather lamely.

"No? But you do about her."

"I wonder. Mavis does strangely fascinate me, I'll admit; but it's Donna that I really care for Dan."

"I wish you didn't," said McGrady soberly. "I think a lot of Donna Cairns. And I'm moving heaven and earth to find some clew toward helping her."

"Well, at least we two have got a common purpose, you and I," said Deane. "But I tell you this, Dan, if I ever disappear, you'll know one of two things: either Maitland has got me, or I've gone to him voluntarily. In either case I'll try and communicate with you."

"Fat chance," said McGrady.

"Both Angus Frazer and Professor Cairns promised to send out word, and you've not heard from either of them. But all that aside, isn't there something we can do now?"

"Just a minute," Deane replied, holding up one finger, and then running his hand through his frowsy blond hair. "I'm about to give birth to an idea. I can't believe that Maitland is out of touch with his old banking firm here in New York. Let's watch the stock market. Why haven't we thought of that before? In the past the movements of the market would have been a clew to Maitland's crimes, for everything he did affected the market, and Maitland always cashed in. So let's watch the market now."

"And let's watch the purchases and sales made by Maitland & Co.," added McGrady.

So arrangements were made for reports on all transactions of that brokerage firm. But for a while nothing developed.

MEANWHILE DEANE'S EXPERIMENTS with stratium continued. One phenomenon intrigued him, namely that stratium would not burn, even in oxygen. All metals will burn in pure oxygen, and some will burn even in air; but stratium would not burn at all. This seemed strange. Everything ought to burn under some circumstance or other.

So, with no particular idea in mind, he tried immersing red hot stratium in various gasses, just at haphazard until finally he tried hydrogen. The result was startling: the stratium burned completely away with a bright blue flame, and yet the hydrogen did not ignite.

Hydrogen, that highly inflammable gas, did not ignite; and stratium, the unburnable, consumed without even an ash! And none of the hydrogen was used up in the process.

He burned more and more stratium in the same hydrogen, until no more would burn. And then he realized the reason. He had combined stratium and hydrogen again into the original stratium hydride of the stratosphere. Stratium, being a negative element, hydridized instead of oxydizing.

And, as his experiments progressed further, he found

a catalyst, in the presence of which the stratium would hydridize instantaneously. Would vanish in a puff of smoke.

All this he recorded in his laboratory notes; but, seeing no practical use for these discoveries, he did not make them public.

At last the spies which had been set on the banking house of Maitland & Co. had something definite to report: the firm was selling bonds, any and all bonds, that is to say any and all gold bonds; and the market began to drop. The financial editors could offer no adequate explanation for the movement, which was counter to all current indications.

And then rumors reached the press that a wizard of chemistry, named Esposatierra, with a laboratory in the mountains of Lower California, had either struck the richest vein of gold in all history, or was extracting it in quantities from salt sea water, or was manufacturing it by pure alchemy, or something. At any rate, this Esposatierra was reported as possessing gold in almost unlimited quantities, and as being about to flood the world markets with it. So down went all gold-backed securities, with Maitland & Co. leading in the sales.

"Well, Dan," said Deane, "here's the news we've been waiting for. But what does it mean?"

"That's what I intend to find out, Charley," replied McGrady. "I've given a rush order to the Luce Press Clipping Bureau for everything on Lower California for the last six months."

"Advertisements included?" asked Deane.

"Say, that's a hunch! Advertisements included." He pressed a desk button, and spoke into the microphone.

"Say, has that wire gone off to Luce yet?—Then add to it to include all advertisements too. And make it snappy."

"I believe we're on the trail of something," asserted Deane.

The clippings arrived the next day from Boston. Most of them proved wholly irrelevant. Many, however, were about Esposatierra and his experiments. But what finally attracted the attention of the two friends was the large number of small want ads, offering work in mines and ranches in Lower California and western Mexico. Several of the advertisements even specified former soldiers, sailors, policemen, rangers and marines.

Soon the wires were humming for information as to Pacific Coast ship-clearances, and movements across the Mexican border. Police in other cities were asked to check up on the employment offices listed in the various want ads.

THE AGGREGATE RESULTS were staggering. Literally tens of thousands of able-bodied men could be traced as having answered the advertisements, and having been shipped into Mexico by rail or boat.

Pushing the inquiry further, District Attorney McGrady found that the phenomenally heavy tourist sleeper traffic of the railroads running into San Diego had been kept out of the press because some one had paid the railroads to suppress the news, and had accompanied the payment by a threat to divert the traffic elsewhere if there should be a leak.

"Very interesting," commented Deane. "But just where does our friend Maitland fit into the picture?"

"I don't know—yet," McGrady replied. "But you can be

sure that all this has something to do with Esposatierra and his gold, and that that has something to do with Maitland & Co., bankers and brokers."

Rumors as to the synthetic gold of the Mexican wizard continued to leak out. The bond market continued to drop, and the stock market to rise.

Reporters tried to penetrate to the wizard's castle, to interview him, but were turned back by well-equipped constabulary wearing the Mexican uniform, it is true, but with white skins, and speaking English perfectly, and Spanish not at all.

The case had gotten too large for Dan McGrady, so he and Deane made a flying trip to Washington, and laid everything that they knew before the Department of Justice. The Federal officials were frankly interested in the kidnappings; but the supernatural angle left them cold, and almost caused them to refuse to touch the case at all.

"Forget it," was their crisp advice, "You two young fellows have been reading too many mystery magazines." Dan McGrady drew himself up, and his blue eyes flashed.

"You can wisecrack me all you wish," he replied, "but I happen to represent the City of New York, and you'll coöperate with her, or take the consequences."

So the Department of Justice put its brains on the case, and discovered that thousands of American rifles, automatic pistols, and machine guns, and millions of rounds of ammunition, which had been sold to parties all over the world, could be traced back to Lower California.

But, of course, none of this got into the press, although increasingly sensational reports of the alchemistical exploits of Esposatierra continued to appear.

And then one newspaper more enterprising than the rest sent an airplane with reporters and aërial photographers down the backbone of the peninsula to see what they could see. They saw! They saw anti-aircraft batteries, and felt them too, for they were shot down in flames, and only one of the crew lived and escaped to tell the tale.

When he stumbled across the international bridge at Tia Juana, and told his story, the United States promptly demanded an explanation from the President of Mexico. El Presidente promptly demanded an explanation from the Governor of Lower California. Whereupon El Gobernado issued a proclamation declaring Baja, California, an independent republic, and himself its chief magistrate.

Señor don Juan C. Esposatierra was named Secretary of State for War, of the new republic.

"And still we don't know where John Cortlandt Maitland fits into this picture," commented District Attorney McGrady.

MEXICAN TROOPS ADVANCING across the Colorado River were hurled back with overwhelming losses. And then a huge silver-colored dirigible appeared mysteriously out of the west, and bombed Mexico City. Mexico promptly recognized the new republic.

So then did the United States, and appointed a Minister to its new neighbor. But still no reporters were allowed. However, one of the Minister's staff carried a concealed camera, and managed to smuggle back to one of the northern newspapers a snapshot of the President of Baja, California, and *his* staff. The newsprint of this picture eventually came to McGrady and Deane from the clipping bureau.

The moment Deane glanced at it, he exclaimed, "Look,

Dan! That fellow standing just to the right of El Presidente. Where have I seen him before. This wide mesh halftone distorts everything."

"I'll send for the original," said McGrady, and put in a long distance call for the editor of the paper.

In due course the photograph arrived, and with it the information, which had not appeared in print, that the man to the right of the President was none other than Juan C. Esposatierra. But to the two friends he was quite some other, for both of them recognized him instantly as John Cortlandt Maitland! Of course. Esposa—mate. Tierra— land. Esposatierra—Mate-land. What a rotten pun!

McGrady promptly communicated with Washington, and had further publication of the photo suppressed.

"I begin to see," said he to his pal, Deane. "A new Napoleon is rising in the west. He 'can't afford to wait' to conquer the world by means of mere piling up of compound interest, and so he has decided to use force."

"And stratium," added Deane, "for I believe that the dirigible which bombed Mexico City was built of my metal."

"You've got considerable on your conscience then," McGrady dryly remarked.

That very night, as Deane was walking home to the apartment which he shared with his superior, he was so absorbed in the latest developments that he bumped into a man in the crowd. Looking up and stammering an apology, he found himself face to face with a hunched-up bearded figure, the very same man who had several times peered in at his laboratory door at the beginning of his strange adventures.

The little man was as surprised at the encounter as he,

but was the first to recover his presence of mind, and duck down an alley. Deane pulled a police whistle from his pocket, blew a shrill blast and followed. Then remembering that he was unarmed, he stopped, and blew several times more.

Out from the alley walked a tall young man, with handsome dark clear-cut features.

"Just a moment," said Deane, stopping him, and displaying his badge. "I am a police officer. Did you see a hunched up old fellow with a black beard run. into this alley just now?"

"Why, yes," replied the man in a pleasing voice. "He ran past me, and then ducked behind some barrels, and squatted down. Want me to go back with you, and help you catch him? I'm always glad to do anything that I can to help the authorities."

"No, thank you," said Deane. "I'm not armed. But here come the police."

TWO OFFICERS RAN up. Deane exhibited his badge, told them who he was, and instructed them to go in and get the old man from behind the barrels, and turn him over to the District Attorney.

"Hurry!" he admonished them. "I've got to push along."

The tall young man was moving slowly off. Deane stepped into stride beside him.

"Hope you don't mind my walking along with you?" said he.

A startled look flitted across the face of the other. Then, "Oh, not at all. Very glad to have you. But why—?"

"Well, the reason is this," said Deane. "In the first place, you're Alpheus of the Immortals. And in the second place,

it's just dawned on me that your voice and the voice of
the hunched old man with the black beard are the same.
I heard his voice once on the street in front of my laboratory building months ago, the day I killed Oscar Cairns,
you know."

"What on earth *are* you talking about?" exclaimed
Alpheus. "I am quite sure that I am neither of the persons
whom you mention."

"Shall we go back and see if the police have found you
behind those barrels?" asked Deane mischievously.

"That wouldn't prove anything. He may have escaped
out of the other end of the alley."

"Oh, no," laughed Deane. "He escaped out of *this* end.
But let's cut out the sparring, Alpheus. I know you, because
I listened to you and watched you for nearly an hour
through a window in Sioux Lodge, North Dakota, while
you argued with Maitland about Mavis, and immortality,
and affording to wait, and—lot's of things. The night before
I escaped. Remember?"

"Then am I to assume that I am under arrest?"

"Not at all. Not at all. Fact is, I'm going back with you."

"To Sioux Lodge?" with a bit of a sneer.

"Oh, no. To Lower California. To John Cortlandt Esposatierra."

"You know a lot, don't you?"

"Quite a lot," Deane admitted, smiling.

All this time, they had been walking on a busy New
York street.

Alpheus shrugged his shoulders.

"All right," said he. "Come along. I'm armed and you're
not. Does that make any difference?"

"Not at all."

"All right. My car's in here."

And he turned into the doorway of a parking garage. A few minutes later, seated side by side in a small coupé, they were driving north, bound for George Washington Bridge.

"And now," said Alpheus, "would you mind telling me why on earth you want to go back?"

"Because I want to see Donna Cairns."

Alpheus almost stopped the car in amazement.

"You mean Mavis Maitland, don't you?" he asked.

"Certainly not! Tell me, is Donna alive?"

"Yes."

"And well?"

"Perfectly well."

"And in Mexico?"

"Yes. She is with her father."

"Thank God!"

DEANE'S TONE OF relieved concern was unquestionably sincere. Alpheus stared at him searchingly, then smiled.

"I don't mind telling you that I was taking you over to Jersey to kill you, for I thought that you were interested in Mavis Maitland. But if it's that Cairns girl you are interested in, then more power to you. I believe that I can use you."

He chuckled as at some hidden joke and then continued, "But remember, no attempt to communicate with that red-headed Irish friend of yours. I'm armed, and you're not."

"Why should I want to communicate? I tell you I'm joining your side."

"And your price? For of course you have a price."

"Naturally. My price is Donna Cairns."

Alpheus smiled enigmatically.

"A pretty big price," said he. "But I'll see what can be done."

A short distance beyond the Jersey end of the big bridge Alpheus turned into a side street and then into a driveway, at the end of which stood a large two-door, two-story garage.

The doors swung open, and he drove in. The other space in the garage was occupied by a large moving-van. Alpheus whistled three times, and two tough-looking men ran down the stairs from the floor above.

"We have company," Alpheus announced to them. "Dr. Charles Deane, one of the two worst enemies of our cause. Tie him up, boys."

"Go ahead," said Deane. "I rather expected this. Naturally, until you find that I'm to be trusted, you don't want to take any chances with me."

Alpheus waited until Deane's hands and feet were securely tied and then casually remarked, "Oh, by the way, I forgot to tell you. Maitland is going to marry Donna Cairns and make her the Empress of the World."

16

MOUNT OLYMPUS

A LOOK OF horror flooded Deane's face.

"But he can't do that!" he shouted. "I *will* go with you."

"Why can't he?" asked Alpheus coolly.

"But Donna is human, and he's—he's—"

"And he's an Immortal," Alpheus completed. "However, Miss Cairns is going to join the Order, you know. Won't that make it all right?"

"Oh, my God!" said Deane.

"You'll do," his captor observed with approval. "But if you'd shown the least bit less evident horror and concern, I might still have had to kill you. For no one is going to be let come between me and Mavis Maitland. Understand that!"

He snapped out these last two words, then turned on his heel and strode over to his car. Deane, with a shrug of resignation, submitted to having his eyes and mouth taped, and his ears plugged. Then he was lifted, and carried, and laid upon a mattress.

Through his earplugs, he could hear the mumbled sound of conversation. Then a motor starting, and doors squeakingly thrown open. And then, he was moving; he was in some sort of a motor conveyance.

A few hours later, the conveyance came to a stop, then

moved on for a short distance, then came to a stop again. Deane's hands were untied, and his eyes and mouth untaped. He looked around. He was inside a large moving van, well up near the roof, on top of a pile of boxes which almost filled the interior. The back doors of the van were open, but all that he could see outside was the starlit sky and the dark forms of trees.

A man, squatting near him, shouted something in his ear, but Deane shook his head.

"Can't hear you," said he. "Wait till I pull out my ear—plugs."

He delayed a moment, to see if there would be objection, and finding none, removed the plugs.

"What I said was," came the pleasant voice of Alpheus, "would you like some coffee and hot dogs?"

"Would I?" exclaimed Deane.

They were handed over in the darkness.

For a while the two men ate in silence.

The meal over, Deane was retaped and retied, and the van proceeded on its way through the night.

17

DONNA AND MAVIS

DEANE SLEPT FITFULLY, the chief trouble being that the ropes on his wrists cut and chafed him, until his hands fell asleep, and that was even worse.

They stopped for breakfast in some thick mountain woods, and Deane was allowed to get out and stretch his cramped limbs.

"Can't you think up some other way of tying my hands?" he complained. "It's likely to take us a week or more to reach Mexico, and I don't know as I can stand it this way. Though I will, if I have to," he grimly added.

Alpheus smiled, but made no reply. Yet at lunch-time he produced a stout leather belt with straps to hold the wrists, and this proved much more comfortable. Also straps on the ankles were substituted for the ropes.

So the trip proceeded, with stops three times a day for meals and exercise. And gradually, the vigilance of Deane's captors relaxed. Yet he made no attempt at escaping, for escape was furthest from his thoughts; nor at communicating with Dan McGrady, for he was unwilling to take the chance. He would have risked his own life, but Donna needed him, and he *must* get to her!

A week and a half later, one night, when Deane's ears

were unplugged for the evening meal, he heard the lap-lap-
ping of waves upon a beach. And when his eyes were
untaped, and he was permitted to crawl out of the van, he
saw a body of water stretching away into the starlit night.
He sniffed the air; it smelled salt. He looked up at the stars,
and observed that the Great Dipper lay at his right.

"Pacific Ocean," he remarked to Alpheus.

"You know too much," was the reply. "Some day it's
going to get you into trouble."

Half a dozen vans and trucks were drawn up on the
beach. A portable field radio had been erected, and at it
a man sat on a camp chair, with headphones clamped to
his ears.

Alpheus strolled over to it, accompanied by Deane.

"Any word from the Cartago?" asked the former.

"She'll be here any moment now," answered the radio
operator. Then, excitedly, "Here's a message from Los
Angeles. The Federals are on their way here!"

Out in the darkness at sea, a boat-whistle sounded.

"Confound that Captain!" Alpheus exclaimed. "Hasn't
he any brains? He was told to douse his lights, and he did.

"But just because no one warned him to keep his whistle quiet, he has to go and toot it. What does he think his
radio is for, anyway?"

"Is that question directed to me?" Deane inquired with
mock meekness.

"What! You here?" Alpheus exclaimed. "Get back to the
van, and tell them to truss you up again."

"Can't I help?" Deane begged. "You'll be needing every
hand to get your cargo aboard before the Federals—
whoever they are—arrive."

*Maitland lay slumped
forward on his desk*

"But you might escape, or gum the works," Alpheus objected.

"And so might I, if I were to start back toward the van, and then slip off into the night."

"Oh, very well."

At this instant there came the crunching sound of a vessel's bow, grounding on the beach; and all hands leaped to the task of rushing the boxes on board. And heavy boxes they were!

As the last box was loaded on, the distant glare of automobile headlights could be seen on the shoreward horizon. Alpheus directed that all his trucks be run down onto the beach in single file, with the leader up to its hubs in the lapping waves. Each car was roped to the next, and a towline was run from the head car to the steamboat.

Then all the motors were started, and the clutches set in high, so that the drive-wheels churned the sand; and the Cartago backed away, turned around and set out for open sea.

A few minutes later, Alpheus gave the command, "Cut!" and the fleet of vans and trucks were sunk without a trace.

Deane reported to Alpheus in the captain's cabin.

"Anything you want of me, sir?" he asked meaningly.

"You did a good job, Jones," Alpheus replied. "I was watching you, and you handled twice as many packages as any of the others. You used to play football, didn't you?"

"Yes, sir."

"Well, remember the three monkeys. Hear nothing; see nothing; say nothing. You can go below now, and find quarters with the rest of the truckmen."

When the sun rose the next morning, they were out in the open sea, with no land in sight. Headed south, so Deane judged by the sun.

Late in the day, they turned east again, and reached a wharf shortly after dark.

Deane was hard at work helping the other men unload, when he heard the familiar voice of Alpheus calling, "Is Horace Jones there?"

FOR A MOMENT he forgot that this was his alias; then he sung out, "Here, sir!" and stepped out of the stevedore gang.

"Wash up, ask the foreman for a coat, and meet me at the dock-office in thirty minutes. We're driving to the capital to-night," Alpheus commanded.

"Very well, sir," said Deane. His meekness was, of course, put on; but why not act meek, if it served his purpose?

The dock foreman gave him a khaki uniform, as well as an olive drab mackinaw jacket. While washing, Deane noticed that, in the two weeks since leaving New York, he had acquired a thick, curly, and quite unattractive reddish yellow beard; so he borrowed a razor from the foreman, and removed it. He was ready on the dot.

Alpheus came swaggering into the office in a more fancy military outfit than Deane had ever seen off the stage. Black leather boots, light blue breeches with wide red stripes, dark blue blouse, black cape with red lining, three silver stars on each side of his collar, and a black plumed cocked hat. His handsome slim figure went well with it.

Deane stared at him with amazement tinged with admiration; and he stared back at Deane with disapproval.

"Who told you to shave?" he barked.

"No one, sir. It was my own idea. If you wanted Donna to see me with that filthy beard—"

"It was not Donna that I wanted to see you that way— But never mind. Come on. Here, Pete, give him a gun; there are still some bandits left in these mountains."

The foreman handed over a seven-shooter on a belt. Deane buckled it on, thanked the man for his many kindnesses, and followed Alpheus out to the car. It was an open car, with a uniformed chauffeur. Alpheus got into the tonneau.

Deane hesitated, then made for the seat beside the driver, but Alpheus called out, "In here, Jones, beside me."

Nearly all night they drove, higher and yet higher up into the mountains, until Deane was thankful that he had been supplied with a coat. Alpheus slept most of the way, with that unbreathing sleep which Deane had learned to associate with membership in the Order. Finally it became so cold, in spite of being summer in the tropics, that Deane took a rug off the rack on the back of the front seat, and spread it over his companion and himself.

But even then he could not sleep. His mind was too full of the two girls whom he was on his way to see at the capital city of Baja, California.

Along toward morning, as they were drawing into the outskirts of a city, Alpheus stirred and awoke.

"Any bandits?" he asked sleepily.

"Alpheus," said Deane. "You know very well that there weren't any bandits. Just why did you give me that automatic?"

"To see if you'd use it on me."

"But if you thought that there was enough chance of that, to make the experiment worthwhile, then weren't you taking an awful risk?"

"Not at all, not at all, my friend," Alpheus laughingly replied, "for, you see, your cartridges were all dummies."

"Hm!" mused Deane. *"Ley fuego* again, eh?"

"Draw your own conclusions," said Alpheus dryly.

The city which they were now entering was quite un-Spanish in its architecture. Concrete construction of the most utilitarian North American style predominated, and the major part of the buildings appeared to be still under construction. The streets were of cement and cinders, broad and well-lighted.

At last they stopped in a brightly lighted plaza, with a fountain and quite newly planted garden beds. With a wave of his hand, Alpheus pointed out a large and pretentious building of Greek design, with canvas draped across various parts of the front, indicating sculpture in the process of construction.

"The Imperial Palace," he explained. "But we stay at the Army and Navy Club, across the street."

Said Deane, "I take it, from your costume, that you are some sort of a General or Admiral, but how can I stay at the Army and Navy Club?"

"You're in the Army now!" dryly quoted the other.

THE CLUB PROVED to be modern in every respect, but new and smelling of fresh plaster and fresh paint. Deane slept the clock around; it was evening when he was awakened by the insistent ringing of his room telephone.

"General Alpheus speaking," said the familiar voice of that individual. "Dress at once, and report downstairs to me."

As soon as Alpheus had hung up, Deane rang the office, and inquired, "Any way that I can get a razor around here?"

"Very sorry, sir," came the reply, "but the General's orders are to supply you nothing without his permission." Deane slammed down the receiver. So Alpheus was determined to make him ridiculous, was he?

Then he said to himself, "Cool down! Hold your horses, old man! Losing your temper won't get you anything. Play the game as Alpheus wants it played, but *keep your eyes open*."

So he dressed, went downstairs unshaven, and briskly saluted his new master. Together they stepped across the brightly lighted evening plaza to the Imperial Palace, where they were shown into a large reception hall.

It was filled with officers in uniform. But among them all there stood out one figure in a plain blue serge business suit, John Cortlandt Maitland.

Ignoring Alpheus, to that person's evident discomfiture, Maitland strode forward and grasped Deane's hand in both of his.

"My dear young man," said he. "I'm so glad that you have decided to come back to us, and even more glad that General Alpheus has assigned you to the Palace Guards. I want to have a good talk with you. But first let me introduce you to the President of the Republic. Here, Castro!"

A fat Mexican, more ornately dressed, and more covered with medals than any of the others, waddled over at Maitland's command. And yet, despite his weight and his ungainliness, it was evident as he approached that he was a personage of considerable character and ability. Deane drew himself together in his most soldierly fashion, and stiffly saluted. Maitland's eyes twinkled.

"Excellency," said he, "this is Dr. Charles Deane, one of the most distinguished scientists of *el coloso del norte*."

"Eet eez one great pleasure," said Castro, grinning in a friendly manner.

Then Maitland led Deane out through a door into a small study, in every respect the office of an American businessman. It was as though a magic carpet had suddenly transported them back to Wall Street.

"Sit down, Deane," said Maitland, closing the door.

"Has it occurred to you that Alpheus is being uncommonly considerate to you?"

"Yes, it has."

"I gave you credit for that much intelligence. Well, it has occurred to me too. We must both watch our step. And now I have a surprise for you." He pushed a button, and spoke rapidly in Spanish into the desk microphone. Then leaned back in his chair, placed the tips of his fingers together, and regarded Deane fixedly with a quizzical smile on his bronzed face.

Presently a door opened, and in walked Donna Cairns and Mavis Maitland, hand in hand. Deane sprang to his feet, and stared in surprise from one girl to the other. The shimmering steely beauty of Mavis Maitland, and the soft brown loveliness of Donna Cairns. Mavis smiled a little, sadly and wistfully, a strange expression for her. And equally strange, Donna stiffened, and drew herself erect with dilated nostrils and flashing eyes.

"Mavis," said her father sternly. "I rang for Miss Cairns alone."

"And here am I too," retorted the girl. "What are you going to do about it, Father?"

THE QUESTION SEEMED to call for no answer; but in any event, Donna Cairns cut in with a scornful, "And so, Dr. Deane, you have gone over to the enemy! They have flattered my father into joining forces with them, but somehow I didn't suspect it of *you*."

"On the contrary, Miss Cairns," Deane retorted, "you *always* seem to suspect me. I came back here because—"

He stopped abruptly, and bit his lip. Maitland was watching him intently.

"I don't care what you came back for!" asserted Donna, belligerently.

"And to think that you came back again, out of father's clutches!" Mavis added reproachfully.

"I don't seem particularly pleasing to either of your ladies, Mr. Maitland," said Deane, with a wry grin.

"Don't class *me* as his!" flared Donna. "I'm not his—yet."

And she turned, and stalked out of the room. Just then the desk-phone rang and announced, "You're wanted outside, sir. A courier has arrived."

"Excuse me, please," said Maitland, stepping through the door into the reception hall.

Mavis made a dash for the desk and threw a switch.

"Quick!" said she. "We have just a moment to talk. This room is wired with dictaphones, but I've shut them off. Tell me, why did you come back? Was it for me?"

Deane gazed into her yellow-green eyes. Something of the glamour of those nights in North Dakota spread over him. But he resolutely shook his head.

Her eyes narrowed, and her mouth became hard.

"Then don't tell me. Please," she begged. "I don't want to hear you say it. I know why Alpheus placed you here. It is because he hopes that you will destroy my father and thus destroy yourself, thereby removing the two obstructions which stand in the way of his becoming dictator and marrying me. I know that one of your reasons for being here is to spy on us. We shall have to take our chances on your being able to communicate with the outside world. But will you give me your promise to protect my father against Alpheus?"

"I will," Deane replied, "if for no other reason than to preserve him for eventual capture."

"I had hoped," said Mavis sadly, "that you would do it for my sake. But the reason doesn't matter. I believe you, and trust you."

She came close to him, nestled her hand in his, and looked up into his eyes.

"And I believe and trust you, too," said Maitland, stepping out of a panel in the wall.

Deane drew away from Mavis, and looked reproachfully at her.

But her father hastened to add, "She knew nothing of that panel. But it only goes to show that nowhere in this whole Republic are conspirators safe from eavesdropping. And now, dear, I want to talk to Dr. Deane."

DEANE STARED AFTER her. When she had left, Maitland motioned him to a seat, and said, "I believe that you and I understand each other perfectly. I expect you to be personally loyal to me and my family. But you are at liberty to spike the Cause in any way that you can. Is that clear?"

"Both clear and generous."

"Don't accuse me of generosity. I'm merely practical. Now, then. You know an uncommon lot about us. For example, you know that it is the use of a synthetic oxygen-producing blood that makes a chosen few of us immortal?"

"So I had gathered."

"And that this blood, this ichor of the gods, has to be renewed periodically, and that Alpheus and I alone possess the secret of this chemical."

"I overheard as much under your window at Sioux Lodge."

"So that's what gave you the clue? I've always wondered. I hope that, in time, you will join our order; but I gather from Mavis that the idea revolts you. So there is just one point that I wish to impress upon you. If the secret should be lost, there is only one way to save the race of immortals; their synthetic blood must be drained off, and replaced by human blood."

"Of the proper classification, I suppose?"

"Yes. And, if not enough of that classification is available, dilute it with normal sugar-salt solution. Draw out a little of the ichor, and then replace with a little of real blood by transfusion; and so on, until the veins are clear."

There was a strange sublimity in Maitland's eyes, which caused Deane to wonder—to wonder uneasily.

"Why do you tell me this?" he asked.

"Because," Maitland replied, "for the first time since I started on my drive for world domination, I feel uncertain of the future. But, if you would join us, everything would be clear."

Deane shook his head.

"I'm sorry, sir, but I can't," said he.

Maitland nodded, with a grim smile.

"I respect you for your quixotic foolishness," he replied. "Well, you are to be one of the Palace Guards. Go and report to the captain. And, for Heaven's sakes, man, get a shave! No wonder the ladies don't like you."

"It's—"

"I know whose fault it was."

"But why not let me go back to my old laboratory job?"

"Because I need guards whom I can trust. Loyalty is better than fear. There are few men under me who would not cut my throat, were it not that I possess the secret of eternal life. As a matter of fact, I trust the men who do *not* belong to the Order, more than I trust the men who *do*. In the early days of the Order, we gave immortality to all comers, which accounts for some of the low grade creatures with ichor in their veins. But now new membership is restricted to those of the highest type. Very few of the rank and file of my soldiery are immortal."

"But I should like—" Deane began.

"You will have plenty of spare time to spend with your friends, Frazer and Cairns," Maitland replied. "And now go to your quarters. Out through this door, and down the corridor until you come to a passageway on the right, marked 'Guardroom.' Oh, and one thing more, Mavis's blood-group is No. 4."

18

THE WAR OF THE GODS

PONDERING THIS LAST remark of Maitland's, Deane made his way to the Headquarters of the Guard, where he was assigned to a bunk, was issued a light and dark blue uniform with red facings, and was given a chance to shave. Then, being told that his services would not be required that evening, he asked the way to the government laboratories. They were close by.

Angus Frazer and Professor Cairns greeted him warmly.

But, "I hear you've both gone over to the enemy," Deane rather scornfully remarked.

"Weel, you seem to be in the same boat, sirr," Angus replied, surveying Deane's new uniform. "And why not! No harm is meant to the worrld, so long as the worrld leaves Lowerr Califorrnia alone. And just look at this laborratorry!"

"I wonder," said Deane, staring around him.

It certainly was a more beautiful and completely equipped chemical laboratory than he had ever dreamed of occupying. He sighed with envy.

"Yes, why not!" added old Cairns, blowing a snort through one side of his drooping moustaches. "Just look at this laboratory! And my daughter Donna is going to become an Empress, if the silly dear will only show a little sense."

Deane braced himself for a surge of resentment at this announcement, but somehow it didn't come.

Then the three scientists sat down and talked shop. All that Frazer and Cairns had to report was that they had been permitted to assist in the preparation of ichor, but that they knew little more of its composition than they had before, except that it contained some self-oxidizing substance, and also some substance for removing the heavy water from the human tissues, all of which they had long suspected. Cairns had taken part in the production of heavy water by the electrical bombardment of certain chemical substances. And Frazer had been permitted to experiment in the search for new neutralizing agents; until, for fear that he was learning too much, he had been abruptly shifted to other work.

"What about you alchemists being able to make synthetic gold?" asked Deane. "The United States newspapers have been full of stories to that effect."

"Poppycock!" snorted Cairns. "I'd expect *you* to believe a tale like that. Maitland has found some rich deposits of gold in the hills, and a new process for extracting it from the ore, that's all."

"But it makes a vurra good prress agent storry, though," added Angus.

Deane then reported on his recent discovery that stratium would burn in hydrogen, and that it would instantly vanish in hydrogen in the presence of a certain catalyst, namely a mixture of nickel and nickel-oxide.

As they talked, a low-tuned radio in the corner played

soft music from some American dance hall. It was hard to realize that they were many miles away from home in a foreign land.

The music stopped, and a voice spoke, "This is Station KFI, presenting the talking reporter of the air. An American warship, blockading the coast of Lower California, has been sunk by—bzt, bzt. Bzt, bzt, bzt."

Cairns switched it off, and dryly remarked, "The censor asleep at the switch again. He'll lose his job, poor fellow."

"What do you mean?" asked Deane.

"Oh, Maitland keeps a man listening on each wavelength all the time. If anything comes over the air, which the populace ought not to hear, the censor is supposed to broadcast immediately a lot of interfering static. This fellow just now wasn't quite in time. We've heard enough in the last few days to be able to piece together what is going on."

"Well, what *is* going on?"

"FOR ONE THING, the State of New York has sent two officers to President Castro, with extradition papers for Maitland."

"That's a joke," interjected Frazer. "They might much better ask Maitland to extrradite Castrro. Forr Maitland is boss heerr, not Castrro."

"But what about the warship?" asked Deane.

"The United States has tried to stop the exportation of munitions, bound for this country; and Castro—that is to say, Maitland—recently threatened to make trouble if they didn't lay off. Evidently they didn't lay off, and so our stratium dirigible sunk an American warship just to teach them a lesson."

"But won't that mean war?"

"What of it? Our one dirigible is a match for all the navies and armies of the world, and we have a second dirigible almost built. It's been tested out with as large as six inch high explosive shells, fired point blank; and they made no impression on it. And the largest American anti-aircraft guns are only *three*-inch."

"What's it filled with?" Deane asked.

"Hydrogen. But the shell is so thick that the hydrogen could never be reached."

"I wonder," mused Deane.

He returned to the palace deep in thought.

The next day, Deane took his first tour of duty on guard, and was assigned to Maitland's private office, where he stood watchfully in a corner, while Maitland received, and talked with, various officials.

Finally, to Deane's intense surprise, Dan McGrady and Inspector Lally were ushered in. Deane was about to cry out to them, when he remembered his position and kept quiet. McGrady glanced in Deane's direction, and raised his eyebrows, but said nothing.

Meanwhile Maitland was speaking.

"Your papers are in perfect condition," said he, "but of course, you must realize the impossibility of granting your request. In the first place, I cannot very well issue an order for my own arrest. And, in the second place, the United States has just seen fit to declare war on us, over a little matter of protecting our own sovereignty. I am afraid that I shall have to intern both of you. You did not come here as diplomats, and so you are not entitled to diplomatic immunity. In fact, you came here on a mission distinctly antagonistic to me personally."

"Of course, my government will protest," asserted McGrady.

"Naturally," Maitland suavely replied. "But meanwhile, so long as you are on good behavior, you can stay in the palace as my guests. Private Deane, escort these two gentlemen to my fiancée, and request her to entertain them."

"Yes, sir," said Deane, saluting.

As he led them out into the corridor, McGrady whispered, "Say, this is a break!"

"Is it?" sniffed Deane. "This whole place is lousy with dictaphones and has a spy system which would put Scotland Yard in the shade. Watch your step, Dan."

Donna Cairns greeted McGrady and Lally with utmost cordiality, but transfixed Deane with an eye of scorn. Then Deane returned to the throne room.

"Were your friends surprised to see you?" asked Maitland.

"Rather!" Deane replied. "But what is all this about war with America? Isn't it a great mistake?"

"Yes," Maitland agreed, "it is. We are not nearly powerful enough to cross swords with your country—yet. We can afford to wait, even though your country did precipitate the trouble. American troops have invaded Tia Juana, and our army is falling back. We've shot down several scout planes. *Ordinary* aircraft is no match for modern artillery."

"No, but *our* aircraft *is*," said Alpheus, stepping out of the sliding panel in the wall.

Maitland wheeled around to confront him.

"I didn't send for you," said he severely.

"No? But I came," Alpheus coolly replied, peeling off his gloves. "You can afford to wait? That's a good one. You, who rewrote the motto on the wall at Sioux Lodge."

"It's no more ridiculous than your becoming impatient," said Maitland. "Why on earth did you strike at America, before we were ready?"

"*I* was ready," Alpheus asserted.

"Were you? Well, I was *not*. Alpheus, you have crossed me for the last time. You are under arrest. Seize him, Private Deane."

Alpheus smiled a meaningful smile at Deane, and indicated Maitland with a slight nod of his head. Deane rose and drew his automatic.

"Now's your chance, Deane. Fire!" barked Alpheus.

In reply Deane pointed his gun squarely at the speaker.

"You are under arrest, General," said he levelly. "Put up your hands."

WATCHING THEM BOTH, catlike, Maitland reached slowly out for one of the buttons on his desk. But Alpheus leaped nimbly to one side, and snatched a pistol from his own belt. Deane shifted his aim and fired.

Alpheus fired back, and the gun dropped numbly from Deane's hand, as his arm hung limp.

Then Alpheus fired point-blank at Maitland, and turning, fled through the opening in the wall. As the sliding panel closed, Deane stooped, picked up his own dropped weapon with his left hand, and pumped his six remaining shots into the wall.

The doors of the corridor and the reception hall burst open, and men came running. Maitland lay slumped forward on his desk, motionless.

Deane stared at him for a moment in horror, then strode over to him. But strong hands interfered.

"Seize him!" shouted the Captain of the Guard. "Seize the assassin!"

"Hadn't you better send for a doctor," Deane suggested calmly. "And you'd better send scouts after Alpheus, before he escapes. *He* is the assassin."

"Nonsense!" snapped the captain. "You were alone with the Chief."

Amid cries of "Lynch him! Lynch him!" Deane was roughly dragged out into the reception hall. Castro came waddling up, panting.

"Wot eez?" he asked.

"This guardsman just shot the Emperor," the captain explained.

"Well, keel heem," Castro commanded. "Wot you waiteeng for?"

"Right here?" asked the captain.

Castro shrugged his shoulders.

"Why not?" said he.

So Deane was backed against a pillar, and his arms tied behind it. A squad of riflemen were told off, and faced him.

More angry than frightened, he shouted, "Look here! Just a minute! Shoot me if you insist, but for God's sake listen to me first. It was Alpheus who shot your Emperor. He came in through a sliding panel in the wall, and went out through it again. You'll find all seven of *my* shots in the wall. If you value the peace of your country, catch Alpheus before he leaves this city."

"Perhaps—" began the captain doubtfully.

"Wot you waiteeng for? Keel heem!" shrieked Castro.

The captain shrugged his shoulders.

"Ready!" He commanded. "Aim!"

"As you were!" shouted a feminine voice, as Mavis Maitland dashed into the room.

The squad sheepishly grounded their rifles.

"What's all the shooting for?" she indignantly demanded.

"This guardsman has just shot and killed your father," the captain hotly retorted.

Mavis paled, stepped back a step, and raised one hand to her breast. Her eyes narrowed, and her mouth tightened.

"Did—you?" she asked.

"Certainly not," Deane replied, looking her in the eye. "Alpheus shot him and escaped through the sliding panel. He got me in the right arm, or I'd have prevented it. I sent seven shots after him, but I'm afraid none of them hit. And these fools here are stringing me up, instead of either attending to your father or trying to catch Alpheus."

MAVIS WHIRLED AROUND and confronted the crowd.

"Fools!" she hissed. "Briggs, you run for the doctor. Here, you two, untie Private Deane. Captain, scour the city, guard all exits, and arrest General Alpheus at all costs. If you find that he has left, send the motorcycle cavalry after him. Is that clear?"

"Yes, Miss," said the captain, meekly.

"Then hurry! What are you waiting for?"

"But I am een command here," began President Castro. "And eet eez—"

"Shut up!" snapped Mavis. "You are *el Presidente* only by virtue of my father's support. Without him you are not even *el Gobernador* any longer."

Castro shrugged his shoulders resignedly.

"That eez why I keel heez assasseen," he explained.

Mavis swayed a little dizzily, and passed the back of one hand across her eyes. Deane, by now released, leaped forward and caught her around the waist with his left arm. His right arm still hung numbly limp.

She shivered, and drew herself erect.

"I must go to my father," said she.

Deane led her into the little office room.

There lay Maitland on a couch, with the doctor bending over him solicitously.

As they entered, the doctor arose and announced, "Bullet through the left lung, and lodged in the back. He'll live unless gangrene sets in."

Maitland opened his eyes.

"Hello, dear," he said weakly. "Did Deane get Alpheus?"

Mavis dropped to the floor beside the couch, and took her father's hand in hers.

"I'm sorry, sir," said Deane. "He pinged my right arm, and I can't shoot very well with my left."

"Too bad," Maitland weakly replied. "You ought to practice to improve your marksmanship."

"There, there, father, don't try to talk," soothed Mavis. "I'll take charge of things until you're better."

"Good little girl!" said he. Then, with a sudden fierceness: "If anyone in this Republic disobeys a single order of hers, they'll hear from me as soon as I get well. Mavis Maitland is Empress for the present. Is that clear?"

He slumped back exhausted, and closed his eyes. Mavis signalled for everyone, except Deane and the doctor, to leave the room. The doctor attended to Maitland, and then bandaged Deane's arm.

LATER ON IN the day, Maitland slept under the influence of opiates.

The Captain of the Guard reported that General Alpheus had escaped to the airport, where troops under his command had turned back the motorcycle cavalry.

At Deane's suggestion, Mavis dispatched Inspector Lally back to the United States with a message, ostensibly from President Castro, to the effect that the Republic of Lower California deeply regretted the sinking of the battleship, that the man responsible for the outrage was now in rebellion, and that if America would keep its hands off until General Alpheus was settled with, Lower California was prepared to make amends and pay a suitable indemnity.

"And mind you, Lally, this is straight goods," Deane cautioned. "No double-crossing. We can do more for the peace of the world by suppressing Alpheus, than the United States can do by compelling us to divide our forces."

Dan McGrady confirmed these instructions.

Mavis also ordered all the army, except just enough to hold the northern passes, to withdraw to guard the capital. But fully half the troops deserted and went over to Alpheus.

The next day Maitland, feeling stronger, insisted on having his bed moved to the audience hall. He approved all that had been done by Mavis during his coma.

"But," said he, "from now on, I'm in charge. As long as I'm alive. I'm going to run this show in person."

He had just been installed, and had been informed of the arrangements for defense of the city, when a messenger arrived from the enemy.

His message read:

PRESIDENT CASTRO
YOUR EXCELLENCY:
   I HAVE NO QUARREL WITH THE REPUBLIC,
BUT ONLY WITH JOHN CORTLANDT MAIT-
LAND, WHO IS USURPING YOUR POWERS. I
UNDERSTAND THAT HE IS BADLY WOUNDED.
GIVE HIM, AND HIS DAUGHTER MAVIS, UP TO
ME, AND THE CIVIL WAR WILL BE OVER, AND
WE CAN PRESENT A UNITED FRONT TO THE
COLOSSUS OF THE NORTH. REFUSE, AND I
SHALL BOMB THE CAPITAL FROM THE STRA-
TIUM DIRIGIBLE. I GIVE YOU THREE DAYS.
      YOUR LOYAL SUBJECT,
            ALPHEUS, GENERAL OF THE ARMIES.

"Want to go, Mavis?" asked her father.

"I should say not!" she replied, with an intense glance
toward Deane.

Somehow he thrilled at the implication.

"Well, Castro," asked Maitland with a whimsical smile,
"are you going to hand me over?"

"But, Excellency," exclaimed the President in a horrified
tone, "eet would be—wot you say—not square shooteeng."

"Good old Castro," murmured Maitland. Then, "But I
wonder what is the matter with the dirigible?"

"What do you mean?" asked Deane.

"Only that, if the dirigible was in shape, he'd be hovering
over the city with it right now."

"I'll find out," said Deane.

So he phoned the secret service. They reported that one of the propellers had been shot off in the encounter with the U.S. Navy.

"That accounts for the three days," remarked Maitland dryly. "Our second dirigible can't possibly be ready in that time. Well, what does someone suggest?"

"I have it!" exclaimed Deane. "Give me a three-inch gun to practice with, and I think I can make it."

So Maitland issued orders to give the young scientist carte-blanche, and Deane rushed to the laboratories. Of course he was terribly hampered by having his right arm in a sling; all he could do was to issue orders, and let Angus Frazer and Professor Cairns do the actual work.

HIS SCHEME WAS simplicity itself, namely to load a three-inch shell with compressed hydrogen, thermit, and the metallic catalyst which he had found so effective in causing stratium and hydrogen to combine. To test his invention, he made a small tank of stratium, with walls three feet thick, to match the bomb-proof walls of Alpheus's dirigible. This tank he filled with hydrogen, to match the contents of the dirigible.

Then he fired his specially prepared shell at it.

The thermit ignited upon contact; but the oxygen, released by the thermit, combined with the hydrogen from the shell, and formed water which extinguished the thermit.

So Deane tried less and less thermit, until he finally had merely the barest trace. This sufficed to ignite the stratium, which, under the influence of the catalyst, combined in a puff with the compressed hydrogen from the projectile.

But only a few inches of the target were burned through before the hydrogen was all used up, or dissipated in the air.

If only the fire could penetrate to the interior of the tank, the hydrogen there confined would complete the process and destroy the entire tank in one burst of flame! But this was impossible. Deane calculated that it would require from ten to fifteen successive hits in the same spot, to accomplish this result.

He needed a larger projectile. But the Republic as yet possessed no guns larger than the three-inch. An airplane bomb would serve admirably. But General Alpheus had all the planes, in addition to the dirigible.

Thus one of the three days of grace passed without results.

And the radio announced that America had rejected the overtures of President Castro and was pressing southward.

19

DISASTER

"ALPHEUS WILL MAKE a shambles of the whole American Army, as soon as he gets through with us," Maitland announced, when this news was reported to him.

"Inspector Lally must have used his own judgment," said Deane, "in spite of instructions from Dan and me."

"Well, he can hardly be blamed," asserted McGrady. "He doubtless thought that you and I were under coercion, and were not saying what we really meant."

"Dan," exclaimed Deane, "you've got to get through the lines to American headquarters and borrow a plane. A big bomber with a couple of empty thousand-pound bomb-cases. If you can make it, we still have a chance."

"Can you trust me, Mr. Maitland?" asked McGrady.

"I can and will, if Deane will vouch for you."

"I vouch for him unqualifiedly," said Deane eagerly.

"Then take my private armored car, and an escort of motorcycle cavalry; and beat it!" commanded the wounded dictator.

McGrady saluted, and left the room on the run.

"The military habit is spreading," observed Mavis, amusedly.

Deane followed, to help with the arrangements, and found Donna Cairns in Dan's arms, just outside.

Deane was enraged and shocked; but, to his own surprise, his indignation was not based on jealousy.

"Donna," said he, "it seems to me that, at a time when the entire Empire of your fiancé is at stake, you might display a little loyalty."

"Dr. Deane," said she, disengaging herself, her face flaring. "I despise you."

"And now, Dan, I hope that this is not a sample of the kind of dependability which you are going to show on this trip."

"I have no explanations to make, or apologies to offer," McGrady retorted; but Deane could see, from the pleading expression in his friend's eyes, that he was saying this to shield the lady.

"I understand," he replied, "and I still trust you. Come on, let's get going."

McGrady flashed him a look of gratitude. A few minutes later, he was speeding northward on his mission, through the starlit tropic night.

Late the next day, one of the motorcycle escort returned to say that Dan McGrady had reached the American lines in safety. The rest of the escort had been waylaid, on the way back, by troops of Alpheus, but this one had broken through with the message.

All day long Deane worked directing the filling of three-inch shells, as a forlorn hope, if the airplane failed to arrive. And by his side worked Mavis Maitland.

"I want to help," said she, "and with your injured arm, you need help. Father's dream of a lifetime is at stake. I want to feel that I have contributed something to keep it from crumbling. And, besides, I want to be with you, close to you. 'To-morrow! Why, to-morrow I may be myself with yesterday's seven thousand years.' Strange, isn't it, how the approach of death makes life seem so much more real?"

"Mavis, dear, I like you like that," breathed Deane.

"What did you say?" she asked, innocently.

"I said, 'Mavis, I like you like that,'" he replied.

"No, you didn't. You said, 'Mavis, *dear*, I like you like that.' Oh, Charles, do you remember that beautiful moon-light night in North Dakota? You loved me then for a few precious moments. But I shall never, never forget the look of horror and loathing on your face when you finally pushed me away from you. Could you love me again, if I were human, instead of immortal?"

"You *are* human," he replied. "We all of us are standing in the shadow of death right now. Your father, one of the only two men in the world who hold the secret of eternal life, is wounded. This city, with all of us in it, is due to be destroyed from the air to-morrow evening. But mortal, or immortal, I love you, Mavis."

"Isn't death a wonderful thing!" she breathed, as he swept her into his arms.

The next day dawned, and still no word from Dan McGrady.

Maitland developed a temperature, but his iron will still kept his mind rational. Arrangements were made to evacuate the city, and distribute its defenders throughout the surrounding mountains, where guerilla warfare could be carried on.

DONNA CAIRNS, VERY contrite, hovered around the Emperor, and seemed to have lost her revulsion for him.

Mavis Maitland and Charles Deane kept close together, and said very little, waiting, happily waiting for their doom.

Around noon the exhaust of a motor could be heard to the northward. Presently the plane itself appeared. Soon the awaiting populace could make out its lines, a huge U.S. Army bomber.

Was its advent friendly or hostile? The anti-aircraft defenses of the city were manned in readiness. And then the defenders noticed a white flag of truce flying from one of its struts. Yet still they took no chances, but remained on the alert. Flags of truce had been but a prelude to bombings in other wars.

By short wavelength radio, a message was sent up, "Avoid the city, or we shall be forced to fire."

Instantly the plane veered off to the westward, circled once, and landed on the habana, just outside the city limits.

It contained Dan McGrady and two U.S. Army fliers. It carried two empty one-thousand-pound bombs. These were rushed to Deane's laboratory, while the two visitors were led before the wounded Emperor.

Dan McGrady loyally avoided a private meeting with Donna.

Deane, with the assistance of Angus Frazer, Professor Cairns, and Mavis Maitland, loaded the huge containers with compressed hydrogen, nickel and nickel-oxide, and a small quantity of thermit. All was in readiness.

"Where are the fuses?" asked Deane.

He had specified *empty* bombs, and so there were no fuses!

Crestfallen, he stalked over to the palace, to break the news to Maitland. Beside him strode Mavis, her hand on his well arm, her face full of concern.

"You did your best, Charles," she urged.

"Yes," he bitterly admitted. "But it reminds me of the old gag about Harvard and Yale. The Harvard coach used to say, 'Do your best, men; and, win or lose, you'll have the satisfaction of knowing that you played the game.' The Yale coach used to say, 'Win, damn yer, win!' So Harvard would do its best, and Yale would win, and everyone—especially the coach—would be happy."

"Don't be bitter, dear," said she. "I don't like you that way."

"But I can't help being bitter. Think what this means to your father! And to the world, for that matter."

"I *am* thinking," said she.

AS THEY ENTERED the huge audience-chamber, where Maitland lay propped up in bed, he was saying to the two American aviators, "And you have my assurance that, if we pull through this crisis, I shall be able to negotiate peace with your country."

" 'When the devil was sick—'" quoted one of the aviators.

"How dare you!" blazed Mavis.

"Gentlemen, my daughter," Maitland introduced, and the two Americans bowed low, while Mavis held her head high, with eyes flashing. Then Maitland continued, "Believe it or not, but I mean it. I've been charged with many crimes, but never with breaking my word. We don't do that on Wall Street."

At this moment a courier came in with another message from the enemy. It read:

TO EX-PRESIDENT CASTRO:

A PLANE FROM OUR NORTH AMERICAN ENEMIES HAS BEEN PERMITTED TO LAND IN YOUR CITY. THIS IS TREASON! I HEREBY DECLARE MYSELF PROVISIONAL PRESIDENT OF LOWER CALIFORNIA.

UNLESS MAITLAND AND HIS DAUGHTER, TOGETHER WITH A DULY NOTARIZED ABDI-CATION BY YOURSELF, ARE TURNED OVER TO ME BY SUNSET, I SHALL START BOMBING THE CITY AT SUNRISE. I PERSONALLY SHALL RIDE IN THE DIRIGIBLE, SO AS TO VIEW THE DESTRUC-TION OF YOUR TRAITOROUS CITY.

ALPHEUS,

PROVISIONAL PRESIDENT.

"The man is crazy!" exclaimed one of the aviators.

"Delusions of grandeur!" added the other.

"Well, gentlemen, let's have dinner," observed Maitland with an airy wave of his hand. " 'Eat, drink and be merry; for to-morrow we die.' Oh, here is Dr. Deane. Well, is everything all set?"

Deane hung his head in abject humiliation.

"I'm sorry to report that I have failed you, sir," said he contritely.

"There are, unfortunately, no fuses for the bombs."

"No fuses?" exclaimed one of the army fliers. "What do you mean, no fuses? What kind of fuses do you want?"

"Supersensitive, a little quicker than instantaneous," said Deane. "But what good—?"

"Got plenty of them. We always carry them loose, and never put them on until we're ready to take-off."

"There, I told you!" exclaimed Mavis, hugging Deane joyfully.

"Ouch!" said he. "My arm!" Maitland raised his eyebrows, then sank back on the pillows with, "The close of a perfect day."

"That's all very well," mumbled one of the aviators to the other, as the party filed out. "But will it work? I always mistrust these college professors, with their bright ideas for improving warfare."

"Well, if it doesn't work," the other replied, "there's one little dirigible afloat that can lick the whole United States. Army and Navy."

After dinner, at which Mavis and Donna charmingly did the honors, the evacuation of the city began. By sunrise the entire population were scattered throughout the surrounding mountains. The few women and children were in caves. The men, disposed strategically. All the available food and munitions were brought out, too.

Shortly after sunrise, word came from lookouts that the stratium dirigible was on its way; and immediately the U.S. Army plane took off, and circled to gain altitude. Soon the silver shape of the enemy airship appeared over the mountains to the eastward. And above it hovered two small scout-planes. *That* complication had not been foreseen.

The scout-planes rose to out altitude the U.S. bomber, and the bomber climbed, too, to beat them to it. Meanwhile the dirigible settled lower, and approached the city.

Anti-aircraft guns blazed away using Deane's specially prepared shells, attempting to register successive hits in the same spot; but all that they accomplished was a slight pitting of the silver shell.

DEANE AND MAVIS, his left hand in hers, stood beside the bed of the stricken Emperor on a nearby hilltop, watching the attack on the vacated city. Maitland's fever had subsided, and he was a bit light-headed, though still he held a firm grip on himself.

The first bomb was dropped on the city, and then the U.S. Army plane dived. Straight down through a rattle of machine gun fire, as she passed the two guardian fliers. Down, down. Then straightened out and swept across the back of the dirigible, loosing the first of its two bombs as it passed.

The bomb grazed the side of its target, and vanished, without sound in a puff of smoke.

Deane clenched his fists. Mavis patted his arm, and snuggled close to him.

"Never mind, dear," said she. "If we go, we go together."

Turning and climbing abruptly with the tremendous velocity acquired by its dive, the U.S. Army bombing-plane made a rolling loop and swept back again. Everything depended on this last bomb, the only one which it had left.

Down toward the bomber dived the two scout-planes, but anti-aircraft fire broke lose about them, and they veered away.

And then the bomber loosed its second and last bomb. Squarely, against the side of the dirigible sped the bomb, nose on. And then the onlookers rubbed their eyes, for there was no dirigible there! Just a blinding flash of silver light, and then a shower of everything that had not been stratium: guns, and bombs, and equipment—and singed cinders that *had* been men!

The bombing-plane swept across the city to the habana. The two enemy planes hesitated, and then flew off to the eastward amid a parting salvo from the guardian artillery.

"Well," remarked Maitland dryly, "the world has been made safe for democracy."

So everyone returned to the city. The charred body of Alpheus was found in a pile of wreckage, and positively identified. Messengers were dispatched to his forces, offering complete amnesty to all who would swear allegiance to the old regime.

But Maitland's fever grew worse.

Along toward evening an ominous crowd began to gather outside the Palace. The Captain of the Palace Guard was about to drive them away; but Maitland, weak though he was, insisted on hearing their grievance.

So the captain interviewed them, and came back to report, and he had an ominous look in his own eye as he did so.

"It's the members of the Order," said he, "and I'm one myself. Alpheus is dead, they say, and they're right in that. There's a rumor that you are dying, too. If you die, we lose the secret of the ichor. They—we—we all beg that you let someone else share the secret, to take the place of Alpheus."

"Quaint, somehow," commented Maitland, with that quizzical smile of his. "Immortals begging a dying man to give them the secret of eternal life."

"It's not so funny, sir," urged the captain. "For God's

sake, name a successor to Alpheus, before you die, and we all perish!"

Mavis stepped forward.

"Can't you see that you're tiring him?" said she. "Your only hope is to let him recover. Leave him alone."

The captain whipped out his automatic, and leveled it at Maitland.

"Give me the secret, or you die!" he hoarsely shouted.

"And kill the goose that laid the golden eggs," taunted the sick man. "What good will it do to shoot me? The secret will perish all the more quickly."

Meanwhile Deane was working his way quietly toward the captain.

"That's no answer," croaked the captain. "Aren't you afraid to die?"

"No!" asserted Maitland. "And if I die, that will be the end of immortality. It has caused too much trouble already on earth. I can see that now. It has cost me and others love." He glanced at Mavis and Donna. Then continued, "It has caused war and many deaths. Let the secret die with me. The world will be better off."

THEN THE CAPTAIN, with a shriek of maniacal laughter, fired. But, as he did so, Deane knocked his hand up, and grappled with him, in spite of the injured arm.

Through the corridors of the palace there resounded the footfalls of an approaching mob, and shouts of "Let us in! Give us life! Give us life!"

The captain's head struck the tiled floor, as he fell, and he lay still. Deane jumped to his feet.

"Quick!" he cried. "Dan, Angus, Professor Cairns,

Castro; and you two Americans, if you will. We must keep them out."

"I'll call the guard," added Mavis. "None of them are members of the Order." And she sped to the guard room.

A motley throng of generals, colonels and other high officials surged into the audience-hall, crying, "Give us life!"

Maitland coolly remarked, "The Titans storm Mount Olympus."

The guard came piling in, fired a few shots, and drove them out. For few of the mob were armed, and all were crazed by fear.

"Search the Palace," Mavis commanded. "And drive all Immortals into the street."

"And," added Deane, "in ease of doubt, scratch the suspect so as to draw blood, and then sniff of the blood. If it smells of hydrogen peroxide, out he goes."

The court physician entered, white-coated, through one of the side doors.

"I am an Immortal, and I stay," he announced, "My one hope is to save the Emperor's life."

"Yes, you may stay, doctor," murmured Maitland faintly.

Finally the Palace was cleared, the doors barred, and the guard posted at all strategic points. Everyone else returned to Maitland's bedside.

The doctor rose from his inspection.

"He has not long to live," he announced.

"The twilight of the Gods," said Maitland, smiling weakly.

Donna Cairns flung herself on her knees beside the bed, and began to sob.

"It's worth dying, to be appreciated at last," said Maitland.

Mavis stood erect and dry-eyed, and suffered all the more, because she refused to submit to her grief. Deane put his left arm tenderly around her, and she did not resist.

Maitland lay with his eyes closed for several minutes; then he roused himself. With the ebbing of his strength, his fever departed, and he was his own dominant self for a brief period.

"Friends," said he cheerfully, "gather closer, while I make my last will and testament, or sing my swan-song, or whatever you wish to call it."

ALWAYS DRAMATIC, HE smiled at the commotion caused by his words.

"Mavis, my little daughter," said he, "to you and Charles I give young love. Also the same gift to you, Donna, and your Dan. Donna, you might have been Empress of the world, if things had turned out differently; but perhaps it is better this way. Dan McGrady, you played square with me, your enemy, by refusing to touch her, so long as she was mine. She is no longer mine, nothing is any longer mine, so take her with my blessing."

Maitland had not known of that one stolen embrace; and this was just as well, for it had not been Dan's fault. McGrady now lifted Donna from where she knelt by the bedside. She turned and sobbed on his shoulder. Maitland gazed after her, long and longingly.

Then he resumed, "To you, Cairns and Frazer, I give the best-equipped chemical laboratory in the world, in the hope that in it you will devise many things of value to the people who followed me into this wilderness."

He paused, and coughed; and a spasm of pain passed across his handsome face.

Then he went on, "To you two aviators, I give a message to your President: a message of eternal peace from the new Republic to the south of you. Ninety per cent of its citizens are of the best American stock: former soldiers, sailors, marines, policemen and rangers, most of them. The ten per cent carry on the traditions of two mighty races: the Aztec and the Spanish."

Again he coughed, and grew perceptibly weaker. Mavis stepped over to him, and took his hand in hers. He smiled up at her, and patted it.

"And to you, Manuel Castro," he continued, "I give the Republic of Baja California. You have been a loyal subordinate; may you prove to be an equally capable ruler. Mavis, dear, you and Charles stay with Manuel and help him. My entire fortune is yours, dear."

He sat suddenly erect, and a distant light filled his eyes. Then he crossed himself, started to mutter a Latin prayer, and fell back on the pillow. The court physician closed the dead man's eyes.

A hush fell over the entire group, to be broken by the sound of a shot. The court physician had committed suicide.

Charles Deane walked slowly away and out through a window onto a balcony. Others were removing the dead physician.

Mavis sat on the side of the bed, her father's cold hand still in hers.

Deane looked down at the milling throng in the brightly lighted plaza below, and a sudden revulsion flooded through him.

"The king is dead!" he shouted down at them. "And he left no successor!"

The mob had halted at his first word. After he finished, they still remained silent for an immeasurable moment. Then there broke from them a wail of unutterable despair.

Some fled, howling. Some beat their heads against the walls. Some groveled on the pavement. Some attacked their neighbors with berserk madness. Those who had firearms, discharged them at themselves or each other, it made no difference.

Gradually the square cleared, save for those who lay dead upon the pavement. Some kind soul turned out the lights, leaving only the tropic stars shining over the peaceful roofs of the city.

"Truly it is the twilight of the gods," said Deane aloud.

A soft hand nestled in his uninjured arm, and Mavis leaned fragrantly against him.

"There is only one Immortal left," said she, "and she alone is not afraid to die. But, Charles, dear, stay very close to me during my last few days."

"Why, Mavis!" he exclaimed. "Didn't you know? Your father told me, before he died, that the ichor can be drained out little by little, and be replaced by natural normal blood again. Why, darling, we have years and years to spend together yet!"

"I'm glad," she said simply, "for I hated to have to leave you so soon. Time is so much more precious than eternity."

www.ingramcontent.com/pod-product-compliance
Lightning Source LLC
Chambersburg PA
CBHW030540030726
47495CB00004B/1066